BLOOD
FIRE
VAPOR
SMOKE

Shann Ray

BLOOD
FIRE
VAPOR
SMOKE

Shann Ray

Attention schools and businesses: for discounted copies on
large orders, please contact the publisher directly. Books are
brought to the trade by Ingram.

For information contact:
Unsolicited Press
Portland, Oregon
www.unsolicitedpress.com
orders@unsolicitedpress.com
619-354-8005

Cover Design: Kathryn Gerhardt
Editor: Rebekah Stogner

ISBN: 978-1-950730-18-6

for Jennifer

PUBLICATION
ACKNOWLEDGEMENTS

Some of the stories in this collection appeared in the following venues, at times in different forms: "Black Kettle" in *Fugue* and in *American Copper: A Novel* (Unbridled Books); "Republic of Fear" in *Salon*; "The Debt Men," winner of the *Pacific Northwest Inlander Short Fiction Award*; "The Current Kings" in *Rock and Sling*; "Love is Blindness" for Humanities Washington *Bedtime Stories*; "Spirit of the Animal" in *New West*; "Fourteen Types of Belief" in *Aethlon*; "Black Wound" in *This Land*; "The Hunger, The Light" in *Five Chapters* and anthologized in *Sandstone*; "Before He Sleeps" in *Northwest Review* and anthologized in *An Elk River Books Reader*; "The World Clean and Bright" in *William and Mary Review*; and "The Beartooth Range" selected by Pam Houston for *Whitefish Review*. I want to thank the editors who placed and helped shape these stories: Luke Baumgarten, Vic Bob, Chase Colton, Dave Daley, Pam Houston, Allen Jones, Janice MacRae, Jeff Martin, Precious McKenzie, Greg Michalson, Scott Peterson, Amy Ross, Brian Schott, and Ye Ye Shen.

CONTENTS

To a grave extent, the transformative power of love is not fully embraced in our society because we have come to believe that torment and anguish are our "natural" condition. Indeed, much of the fear children have to being unworthy of love emerges in their relation to fathers who refuse them acknowledgment and care. "He that feareth is not made perfect in love" uses the masculine pronoun, for collective male fear of love is endangering all our lives and the well-being of the planet. To return to love, to know perfect love, we must be willing to surrender the will to power. It is this understanding that makes this passage from I John so prophetic and revolutionary for our times. We cannot know love if we remain unable to surrender our attachment to power, if any feeling of vulnerability strikes terror in our hearts. As our cultural awareness of the ways love has been taken from us gains recognition, our anguish intensifies, but so does our yearning. The space of our lack is also the space of possibility. As we yearn, we make ourselves ready for the love that is coming to us, as gift, as promise, as earthly paradise.

—bell hooks

Hate cannot cast out hate. Only love can do that. Returning violence for violence multiplies violence, adding deeper darkness to a night already devoid of stars.

—Martin Luther King, Jr.

THE SOLACE OF BEAUTY

—foreword, by Noy Holland

In Shann Ray's marvelous collection, *Blood Fire Vapor Smoke*, the stories are often linear, and the narratives ascend in a dramatic arc. The beauty of the language, the collection's historical range, and Ray's reach for—sometimes prayer for—mercy and compassion in the face of horrific violence, his insistence on the solace of beauty, make this a brave and worthy book of stories. I find the collection riskily unclassifiable; it feels restless, not just because it moves among different physical settings, but because it moves from what can read as historical fiction to an intimate and contemporary mode, and because Ray works to see a driving masculinity prismatically.

This restlessness, the unwillingness to conceive of a singular answer to the question of what nourishes the appetite for violence—in the kitchen, in theatres of war, in alleyways, in ravaged cities—across the centuries and across continents, is true and inventive. The collection becomes a genuine inquiry in which salvation and damnation, wickedness and blessedness merge—a hard book to write, hard won, and risky.

Blood Fire Vapor Smoke has some sensual and topical similarities to Stephen Graham Jones' *Ledfeather,* though Ray's collection is not as dreamy and disorienting. James Welch's *Winter in the Blood* feels relevant too—in its eloquence, and its braiding of tribal and familial history. In some of the omissions and syntactic turns, I hear echoes of Cormac McCarthy's work. I have a soft spot for stories that unfold in the rural west, and there is plenty of Montana in this collection. Ray animates the landscape, presents and valorizes the catharsis of physical labor, and sees the sublime of open spaces. I like fiction that gets out of the city and there's hardly a trace of the urban contemporary here, and hardly a trace of anything wry or hip or ironic. Ray runs against the grain of what gets picked up and celebrated in a commercial milieu.

Onward.

I am drawn to the sensual charge of the physical world here—muscle and rock and river. Ray has a gift for description. His love of the plains and Rockies is abundantly apparent, but his gift of description is itinerant, too, as in the story "The Diplomat", set in a desolated city in a fractured Africa. Ray moves nimbly between the human body and the texture of the natural world, in an expression of longing that will have no answer he writes of "a moisture to the skin… like the leaves outside the office window at the embassy, lush and inviting." Folly and arrogance are operative, in both the national and the individual sphere. We watch the circle of violence close in on a failed and failing American diplomat who is by turns paralyzed and animated by desire for a young boy seeking mercy. Mercy belated, mercy refused. Ray does not indict; he moves into whatever light he can find, taking care to observe the small creature and at once the great expanse. The story ends with the exultant image of a flock of white flamingoes taking flight, and "…at last the travelers made out the stars that wheeled overhead like a silver river harkening them on."

In "Republic of Fear" a grandfather mutilates his grandson in a hidden Libya, sending him out to avenge the death of the boy's father. Revenge motivates the Cheyenne warrior in the story "The First Man" and although this is a story whose principle mode is action—a narrative of pursuit with the intent to kill—it is also an inquiry into the nature of revenge. Another story emerges from the Sand Creek Massacre, in which the cut away genitals of dead warriors are paraded on the stage of the Apollo Theater in Denver. This story is accompanied by other stories of the Cheyenne in prison camps, counting coup on the plains in the 19th century, playing championship basketball in the 20th/21st century—stories of genocide and institutionalized racism in which Ray finds reprieve in loyalty and beauty.

In "The Debt Men" the hungry, the glutted, the full of life and half-dead are center stage—a couple of degenerates undone in the parking lot of the Safeway in Spokane. Ray includes a story of WWII, and one of a Montana couple—a ballet dancer, and the son of a brutal alcoholic—navigating marital infidelity. The more private stories are often sorrowful and tender, and it's here where I find the line most definitively drawn between sensation and sensationalism, sentiment and sentimentality. A real attentiveness shows in compression, as with this description of a boy's mother: "His mother was made of needles. Below belief, intimacy, he thought. Below severity, fear."

The stories in *Blood Fire Vapor Smoke* are sophisticated and smart, and at times rich with allusions to Kafka, Jung, Rankine. In the tales set in the 19th century in particular, Ray enriches by the vernacular of myth. Here's an example of this richness, and I'll end here: "He closed his eyes and fell inward and down into a sleep that came like a pall draping the body whole, Cheyenne territory: cold night, bright bone, hot blood from the skull, down his neck. I am made of paper, he thought. He turned and faced the animal."

I was overcome by the power of these stories.

I am so glad this book has found a home with Unsolicited Press.

BLOOD

Flesh and blood needs flesh and blood, and you're the one I need.

—Johnny Cash

THE FIRST MAN

THE FIRST MAN ran north hard under cover of night, fast along riverbed and up climbing the forested bulk of land over land, up rock faces and out upon the serrated edge of snow-laden cirques and down again descending into valleys and further down low upon the valley floor, into a daylight that pierced all as he ran through pinch of canyon walls and out again over open plains crumbled at the far edge by timber and stone, down in the night to the heart of the great forest and out finally over a wide expanse of grey rock, bold line of trees along the Big River below, the man who ran more animal or wind than man, bent to the far place of snow and skyborne earth, bent with abandon to Ten Mountain House.

Like shadow the second man followed the first, desiring him dead.

To the house of the sun the men traveled, one sighting the mark of the other, depression in snow and bitten branch, grasses laid low among that which the wind has lifted and set down again, dirt, leaves, snow, a hint of thornberry in the air and with it the scent of wood smoke. At the fjord of Two Rivers Plateau, behind the cliff wall of the Beartooth escarpment, a valley opened and from the high ridge to the north, the second man, broad-shouldered, hailed the first.

"Hail now, listen! I see you with my own eyes and you are well made and I have great sorrow. For you must die. And I must kill you."

The voice carried, low and full of feeling, and the first man stopped and paused, and turned his head, and sought the form of his enemy far off atop the grey stone. Seeing his once-friend he put his fist to his chest, then pointed upward where the ball of fire burned, covering half the sky. He yelled with great feeling:

"I am like the sun. I will never die!"

Then he ran into the forest, hidden as he followed the river south.

HORDES OF MEN desolated, struck down, destroyed, sunken form of skin and bent skeleton, bare hide matted to torso, bodycage and hipbone, face and neck darkened, bloated to black, rain the endless dream stuck fast in the stone-dead skull and blood a fine sheen over all, arms and legs tangled, a severed hand, eyes dull white opals half-bled from orbital bones, grey earth below and stink in the air and the near cry of scavenger birds, birds of unbearable hunger, the sodden smell of open wounds, a flock of dayraven far above, black, and in the blackness light, black sky with stars and moon like fires defined wholly apart from one another and only darkness in between, mute beacons, and cold. The sun had gone and there was near silence after seven nights of fighting, and in the quiet only the caw of birds and the faint word, like a child's, of those whose breath, impatient, labored, stops, and broken off, takes leave to await them in spirit or etherworld, blood echo in the air, agony awaiting peace on the other side.

Hordes of the first clan in the second clan's darkness, the first and the second come to kill over fear and vengeance and love.

In the end all were blind, or maimed, or dead: save two.

He, the first. The second, his once-friend.

THREE NIGHTS MORE, a closer, more circular and predatory pursuit.

The first man, unable to shake the one who stalked him, turned south and east, and led him away from woman and child, away from a desolation he felt assured would accompany his own death; so he went south and shunned night omens, and waited for the morning star, and prepared to take the life of his friend. Unafraid. Afraid. Continuance, longsuffering, movement, in old seasons savage attacks in darkness or dawn, him to the other clan, the other to his own—these he had visited upon others, and others upon him. He was tired. He would end everything today.

In the half-dark he rose and pressed dirt from the riverbed through his hair, the soil oily and blue-black, gritty, a surface of muddied silt he applied equally to his face and chest and forearms. He would be of the earth, he would rise from the earth, to the earth he would return. He had seen no birds the previous day, another night omen. He lay with his back to the earth, body outstretched, he prayed to the sky before light, to open and give him the sign he sought.

At first light, the sign, but darker still. Dayraven, the Life Eater, high above, small as a thumbnail to the eye, circling the open rock face on which he lay.

He tried to ignore the sign and rose from his place and went and hid himself, prostrate in a stand of willows, to await the other. Once-friends, brothers, the families had parted, he could not remember when, some seasons past, over the accidental death of an elder. Powerful elder, the Old One, he who the second man claimed the first had played a part in killing. The death of the elder had become an excuse, the first man thought, for the second to do what he wanted—seize more than the allotted share, wield what he seized like a weapon. The first man had wanted peace, and he reasoned there was a time when the second agreed, but finally nothing came to them for which to make an appeal, neither kindness nor regard, nor good will, nor spirit, nor even the quiet tenderness that in their youth had so long been with them, the former life now a whisper hardly heard or recalled. Of the darkness, no light, and of the light no sign or symbol, the heart of man awaits light like water poured into that which holds all autumnal, liminal. On the threshold of death he sees trees let go their leaves and stand naked against all as into the hard ground the light descends and there where dark holds sway, water conducts every latency upward and springs forth, once-interred and held womblike, but given again to go from land to a height of sky unforeseen and glint upon upturned leaves, and higher, setting gold on the back of the dayraven.

But light eluded them, and death not life, became them. Death without water, without soil, the soul in its dark raiment walking the earth vacant-eyed, alone.

Concealed among willows at the bank of the river, the first man turned and lay face down, still as stone. Today he would kill his friend or be killed. He hoped in the first, but welcomed the future, be it success or his own ending.

THOUGH THE THOUGHT of taking the first man's life broke him the second man came on. I will make a new start, he reasoned. The clans were decimated, his clan and the first man's. There would be just one clan now, and of a new name, to cleanse the old. First the first man must die, then the second man and the women warriors and the very young who hadn't fought could be at peace and make a fresh path.

THE SOUND of heartbeat in his ear, the first man woke, his face pressed to his forearm. The mud had dried and from a distance he heard feet that ran on stone, the sound a beautiful rhythm over huge teethlike rocks that met the river on the far side, rock borne of a massive slide from before the known world, rock marbled and open that rose from the river outward and up, giant rock wedges and cleavings set far back into the forest.

In among the wood, the sound drew nearer, the feet of his enemy come to harm and to kill. Silent, the first man drew his body upward to a crouch. In the hard slant of sun he saw the open rock towers, and emerging then upriver the body of the second man like a strong animal running, animal and man, legs that drove hard as he traversed, very fast, an uplifted arm of stone, where he met the apex and gathered and leapt high and far, wide-armed, back-arched, diving to the river below. The first man watched the flight of the second and felt joy in his heart as the second man pierced the water, and when he finally surfaced the first man saw the second work to the near side of the river, and again, as in their youth, he loved him.

He kept himself concealed and watched the second man emerge, stone knife in hand, on the near bank just north, and very near. The first man held a rock club to his chest, the flexible handle leather-bound, comfortable and warm in the palm of his hand.

The second man shouted, "*Nah-shluhdahnoh!*—I say goodbye because I know, once-friend, you are here!" The second man stood, feet wide, hands on his hips, looking off west, away from the first man, smiling. "I smell you, once-friend. I have come to see you join the dead."

The first man bolted hard for the second man, and the second turned to him as the first raised the club and swung a mighty arc, striking the second man on the side of the head.

The second man recoiled and rolled with the blow and thrust upward and out, embedding his knife in the gut of the first. Swift motion, and firm, the second man carved a single sweep, moonlike, deft from the seat of the pelvis, left-side, lower body, full to the rib-work, rough-hewn hilt of blade that tilled the body cavity, a thrust-point separating the first man from himself.

The attack was mutual and resolute and of such force both men stumbled and fell bone to bone in a heap on top of each other. Blood bled from the second man, the side of his head scooped out, large divot above the ear, the skull showing and among the blood a dent of flesh and fractured bone depressed but not wholly crushed. And from the first man, a river of red passed down from the vessel of his body into the earth to darken the earth and deepen it, and from his mortal eyes the light lifted and went out.

THE SECOND man stood and felt at the broken part of his skull, and wiped blood on his legs. He went to the first man and knelt over him. He closed and kissed the first man's eyelids and wept.

With the sun past the zenith, he rose and walked along the river to Ten Mountain House where at a great height he found her. The woman, her freshly-awakened child, three-cord weave of rawhide in her hand, as she waited to strangle the child, then slit her own throat with the longknife, wood handle, crude stone sharpened narrow and longer than the foot of a man, a blade meant for cleaning deerskin and carving meat for cooking or drying. She was ready, but unaware as he crept silent behind her from the forest. He saw the glint of her hair, the hand like a stone door over the mouth of the child, small boy-child of perhaps three or four winters.

The man leapt quickly and took her weapons and kissed her hands and she was heavy with loss and rigid with violence and aware he was her husband's enemy. In that moment also she saw her child, the boy's long hair and open eyes, and she kept her words quiet and watched the second man. She noted the bruises on his face, the black wound above his ear by club or hammer, and about his body the colors of soil and silver river and war. In his eyes he bore great sorrow.

Her look questioned him of the others, the men.

"Not one," he said.

"None," she whispered, and she rose and took his hand in hers and led him to the stone hut with wooded roof and center fire, and she lay the second man down to sleep. And as he slept she touched his wounds with water and remembered once he was called brother to her clan, brother to the first man. She kissed the underside of his wrists and at the end of her work she drew the child close and lay down with her child in the angle of the second man's body, and she was consumed with thoughts of death and yet she lived. She lived for her child, and for that which unnamed, yet breathes, alive and vital in all.

REPUBLIC OF FEAR

"YOUNG ONE, do you know what to call me?"

The old man nearly whispered the words, his mane of hair in loose curls, head down, knees wrapped in his arms. The face now, the reporters proclaimed, had become the mask of a clown, long and drawn, creased, darkened. *Gaddafi Fallen...* *Libyan Despot Deposed... Gaddafi Hunted...* the news ticked in his head. But the ease with which he countered it amused him. He lifted his eyes. I am the hunter, the Colonel thought, they the hunted. He and the child were in a black box, a small space six feet by six feet in the middle of the city. From the seams where the wall met the ceiling, light pierced the room forming a rectangle of fire in the blackness. The sun at 12 o'clock overhead, he reasoned. The heat. The reek. They'd been here seven days undiscovered. His own secret cell, an encasement he'd made for himself a decade ago set three floors up in the density of the city, 12-foot-deep concrete walls, hidden in the midst of all. Fortified steel anchored the room to the ground two floors below. The roof was made of simple tin because he'd channeled the money elsewhere then forgotten to return to the project until it was too late. Air vents, small propane cook stove, a bed, water, low bidet, open hole, no nurse, no tent, nothing else now but the boy, and the body of the boy's father in the corner of the room covered by a blanket. The boy's father had died two days ago. No radio, no contact. The Colonel hadn't yet planned how or when he might emerge. Not now, he knew, but when?

Walls tight as the den of a jackal.

He'd owned this country. But his enemies had ousted him, and for now the coup was successful. He would steal their zeal though, he thought, return to power like a thief in the night, torture their women and children, make them watch as he slit their throats, carve out the eyes of the men and starve them, burn blood memory into their skin.

The room had everything but a roof he told himself, the tin overhead not strong enough to repel a simple bullet. But who cares, he reasoned, no one knew where he was. They could search all they want. He'd come here in the chaos, with no time to even gather food. And the place was not pre-stocked correctly. There was only water, gallon jugs that lined the walls. Thin ceiling from which to emerge through a small square opening when ready, secure enough to ward off enemies, secure enough for concealment, but like a tomb, he thought. His own sarcophagus. A missile from above would erase him from existence. But no one would think of him here in the middle of everyone, among over a million people, and they wouldn't kill their own, that was the difference between he and the West, the white press like pigs lapping the birth blood of their young, cleaning the mouth and nose for breath. They'd be tracking him with their agents, their dogs, that and manning the waters like fools in their little boats.

He'd wait them out right here.

The boy was silent, his small arm locked under Moammar's, child hands gripping the man's bicep. Moammar spoke aloud now. "Do you know what to call me, little one?"

"No, Momo," the boy said.

"Call me the King of Kings," he said. A joke. Not as funny as it once was. He pushed his hair back and stared at the boy. The only one left to him now, his first son's youngest, first son from the Colonel's second wife Safia Farkesh, his first son dead on the floor in the corner of the room. The boy was the newest grandson. Called Saif after his father. Everyone was dead.

The boy turned and placed his head on his grandfather's lap. The Colonel dreaded the next step. Nothing for it though, he told himself, he would commence with it tomorrow and it would be done. The boy must survive and get to exile, and return as a man. He had thought he would do it today, but instead, now that the light waned, he took the boy and lifted him in his arms and kissed the boy's face, his cheeks and lips, and carried him to the bed and lay down with him until the boy slept and the Colonel rose and returned to the floor and held his knees in his arms and stared straight ahead.

The following day, near night, he heated the cooking pan. He gripped the boy's wrist and forcefully drew him to the floor. He pressed the boy's left hand to the concrete, raised the knife and cut off the last joint of the boy's pinkie finger. The boy yelped with pain and fear and clutched the hand as blood welled from the hole and darkened his forearm. The Colonel took the boy's hand then and pressed the open wound into the burning pan on the stove. He held the boy, the body squirming, shrieking. The Colonel gripped and pressed more firmly as the flesh burned. The boy let out an animal cry and fainted and the Colonel held the boy to his chest, stood and sat on the edge of the bed, holding the boy to his chest.

Further on the boy woke, whimpering as his small body heaved and sound emerged again like a siren from his chest.

"Remember this," he spoke in the boy's ear. "This cutting, this burning… they did this to your grandfather, the King of Kings." The boy's screams became sobs as he huddled against his grandfather's chest. The Colonel carried the boy to the body in the corner of the room then, pulling back the blanket with the knife and showing the boy his father's face. "Remember this," the Colonel said. "This they did to your father." He leaned and touched the lips of his dead son, then touched the boy's lips. "Avenge your father," he said to the boy. "Avenge me."

He covered the face again and carried the boy away from the body toward the bed. The boy clung to him like a fierce creature. He pulled the boy from his chest and held him up and looked into his eyes. "You have my strength," he said. "Survive."

"Fear Allah that you may prosper," he said. "God is with those who persevere."

He draped the boy on his back. "Hold my neck tightly." He carried the boy up the wall ladder to the hole in the ceiling where he worked the lock and opened the trap door and rose until his torso was clear. There he drew the boy forth, setting the boy out on the surface alone.

"Go," he said, and the boy fled, frantic and ungainly, holding his hand to his chest as he ran across the rooftops into the city. The Colonel watched until the body merged with the darkness and was gone.

Then the Colonel closed the trap door, set the lock, and descended the ladder. He took the knife from his belt again and walked and lifted the foot of the blanket in the corner of the room. He carved two long strips from the calf muscle on the right leg of the body. He returned to the stove and set the strips in the pan. So little time now before the body would sour and the meat would be inedible. Carved thin, the cooking would not take long. The smell was something akin to incense and wild boar. The smoke fed itself into the air vents and disappeared. The Colonel turned the stove off, took the pan and sat cross-legged on the floor. The meat, he carved into small pieces. "Flesh of my flesh," he said, and fed himself.

When he was filled he leaned his back to the wall and closed his eyes.

When the room was black he went to the bed and slept and did not dream.

BLACK KETTLE

A Triptych

He knows what lies in the darkness, and light dwells with Him.
—Daniel

I. BLACK KETTLE'S DREAM

1864.

A YEAR fresh from the century of enlightenment. A year in the cauldron of civil war. In a time of severity and struggle, Black Kettle, chief of six-hundred Cheyenne, led his people following buffalo along the Arkansas River of Kansas and Colorado. They passed through the scablands of the north, rock outcroppings and veins of sage, swells of sparse grass that led finally to land broken by coulees where a few thin cottonwoods remained even in dry dirt. The trees looked barely alive, waiting on storms and flash floods, roots like slender fingers seeking water in the underground and Black Kettle saw their withered form and continued on from there and brought the Cheyenne to Big Sandy Creek in the Colorado territory. Though they had no signed treaty, he and his people relied on good will and camped with the Arapaho near the white man's outpost called Fort Lyon, where he meant to make peace and accept sanctuary.

IN THE WEST, Colonel John Chivington, his family having immigrated to America two generations before, raised the Third Colorado Cavalry with rough-hewn force, hodge-podge militia mixed equally of drunkenness and the wish to kill. Chivington led a band of 700 men into Fort Lyon and gave notice of his battle plan against the nearby Cheyenne encampment. Although he was informed that the Cheyenne under Black Kettle had already surrendered, Chivington left the garrison and directed his men to pursue Cheyenne extinction.

BLACK KETTLE lay in his lodge on a bed of sagebrush covered with robes, warmth of his wife like a bird in the palm, and he remembered in former days how the band asked to be brought as blood into the White Man's family. He was a young soldier chief then and as he listened to the head chief he'd thought the request very wise: the chief asked the White leaders for one-thousand White women given as brides to the Cheyenne, to unite the Cheyenne with the White Man. The White Man, haughty, refused.

Lying still, Black Kettle saw night overhead through the tipi opening and remembered capturing eagles as a young warrior to gather emblem-feathers for the peace chiefs. Now I am an old chief myself, thought Black Kettle, and he remembered how with singular hatred the White Man had said no to the Cheyenne request for White wives.

He whispered to his sleeping wife, "An eagle can take in nearly the whole world with his eyes and know it as clearly as a man looks at the ground by his feet." In this way Black Kettle saw the heart of the White Man, and saw it was dark. Still he hoped in the good of all men, for an end of fighting and the beginning of new days.

Black Kettle's camp meandered along the Big Sandy, 120 lodges, people of skeletal hunger, sunken eyes and burnished skin, near dead, he thought. For them he held both hope and great despair. He remembered a time when dogs licked antelope grease from the tips of his fingers and he rubbed his hands in the scruff of their fur. There were no dogs now. Everything seemed to be made of starvation and war.

In the darkness he rose and walked among the sleeping lodges. He passed the lodges of Elk Society Headsman Standing In Water, Kit Fox Headsman Two Thighs, and Yellow Shield, leader of the Bowstrings. He passed the lodges of Chiefs Yellow Wolf, Warbonnet, Sand Hill, Bear Tongue, Little Robe, Bear Man, Blacktail Eagle, Spotted Crow, Bear Robe, White Antelope and One Eye. A strong village once, but now with so much hunger Black Kettle's sorrow was heavy. He had fought wars with the White Man at Fremont's Orchard, and Cedar Canyon, and Buffalo Springs, where the soldiers killed Chief Starving Bear. He had made raids along the overland routes and killed the Hungates at Box Elder Creek and killed Marshall Kelly and captured his White woman Laura near Little Blue River. But the White Man only increased in number and took more Cheyenne lives. He walked the full length of the village along the north side of Sand Creek and heard the sound of the river and no one rose to greet him and he was glad of it. He sang his chief's song for he would do a good thing and he decided he would do this thing tomorrow; he'd take the people all the way into the White fort and make peace so they might receive food and not starve.

The time now was not the same as former times. It wasn't like when Wolf Tooth and the Cheyenne made peace with the Utes. Then they just came together, and each man chose a friend on the other side and gave him gifts, clothing, and moccasins, and a horse or two. Wolf Tooth had gained a Kiowa friend the same way, who gave him a strong horse and some beautiful clothes, and those good moccasins the Kiowas wore with leather soles all in one piece and fringes on the heel and on top. Wolf Tooth gave the Kiowa man all his best clothes in return, and an excellent war horse he hated to give up, but he was happy to have a friend in the tribe they used to fight. The Whites were different. They gave as a group, clothing and calico and flour and sugar and coffee. One time they butchered a hundred head of cattle by a river, but the White men let the meat set too long and the Cheyenne never touched those carcasses and just let them rot. The meat tasted funny and sweet and they wouldn't eat it.

At the end of camp Black Kettle stood and watched the river for a great while. In a meadow across the water One Eye's black-white paint, a horse fast and fearless, stared back at him. Black Kettle returned to his lodge and lay down and drew his wife near again and held her as she slept, and he waited for sleep.

Deep and dark the dream. Darker the waiting day.

II. CHIVINGTON'S TREACHERY

BLACK KETTLE raised an American flag and a white flag of peace over his tipi.

Chivington raised a hand to quiet his men.

He sat astride a big-haunched pale horse on hardscrabble dirt under the gray pre-dawn sky. He was a man of thick face and eyes, small ingrown beard and wide nose, overly fat and pink-skinned like his father, far son of those unknown to him. Chivington positioned his men, along with their four howitzers, around the Cheyenne village of Black Kettle.

"Remember boys, big and little, nits grow up to make lice. Kill them all."

Children, child-wealth to the Cheyenne but to Chivington, a deacon, a Methodist clergyman, the Cheyenne children were vermin and less than dogs, worthy only to die, and worth less than his words of dispatch, and barely worthy, he thought, of the time it took to kill them.

Scream of gunfire in the waking hour. Shouts of warriors and wails of women, children awake and running in the pale half-dark over the surface of the water, to the far side of the river, the river a small barrier between the charge of the White Man on foot and horseback, the soldiers fat with bloodlust for the ill-prepared, small band of warriors who put up return fire of bow and arrow and some few guns, to make time for Black Kettle to move with those he could and follow the children through the water to the other side and take the far bank, seeking cover.

Behind Black Kettle the sleeping woke to bullet fire and White men walking like darkness painted pale, the point of knife and hatchet blade and butt of axe, bayonet and big guns in smoking towers rolled on wheels, spitting fire on the body of the Cheyenne, herds of guns issuing malice and burning lead through flesh and bone.

Below him in the riverbed, Black Kettle's wife fell, shot multiple times in the back, and he thought her dead, and fell silent, watching. Beyond her body, he saw the White interpreter George Bent with his wife Magpie, Black Kettle's own niece. Magpie behind him, Bent emerged from his lodge near the southern point of camp. Hands raised, he waived his arms. "Stop!" He yelled. "Halt!" But the White men pushed him aside and walked over him and Black Kettle thought how like a windblown young tree the man looked, bent to the ground, arms pale, leaning off to one side. He saw the hands of the attackers in hard circles in the air as they struck children and killed them, shot old men and kneeled in fierce strokes over women, the White men with vigorous knife-work who sawed roughly and desecrated the dead.

Turning, Black Kettle faced uphill and shouted, "Fly! Keep alive! We gather after nightfall!"

CHIVINGTON RODE engulfed by those well-armed and drunk on liquor and blood, rushing down on those who asked for restraint but who garnered only his measure of hate, his method borne of the small heart, unfit and rabid. After a day of war, he wanted victory, no prisoners, and the cannons and rifles pounded the Cheyenne, and as the tribe scattered in panic many were hunted down and shot. Soldiers charged, and killed all that moved. The group of Cheyenne warriors holding the river ran through the water and up the hillside. They followed the few who escaped. Near the far bank a single dead tree, white as bone and nearly limbless, stood in stark contrast to the black of the water. A lantern moon, full and dirty, hung low in the early dark and touched the land with opaque light. Over the battlefield, winds sent a flock of black swifts swerving. They banked upward along the river and fell away, reckless with speed.

STILL DARK. Light-burn on the edge of the world. Into dawn's light Chivington cantered as dust rose from the ground and bullet fire banged like hard rain around him. He led the men forward with their howitzers, up the river bed to kill those who tried to escape. The remaining Cheyenne, mostly the old and the weak, the elders, the women and children, dug small trenches in the ground, sand pits in which to conceal themselves and use what meager weapons they'd taken hurriedly from camp to counter the onslaught.

Chivington pressed forward with the Howitzers and laid down suppressing gunfire. He blew the people from their moorings. When everything grew quiet he stopped and held up his arm and again his men halted. He dismounted and took them on a tour of the dead over which he held himself and jerked each head taut, woman, child, man, and carved away their hair and opened their deerskin clothes and set his hand on their genitals and scalped women's pubic hair and carved away breasts and took the genital skin of boy and man to use and sell, coin pouches for the privileged, fine place, he thought, to carry what economy a man might have. He'd share with those Denverites he knew would turn a gleeful smile. The men followed him, and spat epithets, and gathered what they willed as they ran with curved backs and took as he took and carved as he carved. They pocketed grotesque treasures and laughed aloud and choked on laughter, busy building frenzy to nightfall when they gathered and built their fires, their conflagrations that licked like tongues, phosphorescent orange and red in the hovering dark.

34

OUTSIDE on the long night the remnant of the Cheyenne smoldered on the plain, largely alone, and still. Finally, they rose and moved and found one another like vapor, like smoke, children of the day who bore silently the massacre that turned women to warriors and made every Cheyenne man pledge his life to kill the White Man.

SEE ONE woman. Black Kettle's wife. Shot 9 times. Left for dead, Black Kettle took her up and carried her and found refuge in the camp of the Cheyenne Dog Soldiers at Smokey Hill River. She lived, and from that day forward she was called Woman Here After. The rest who survived also joined the Dog Soldiers, and Black Kettle led them and lay down with his wife again in the healing lodge.

SEE THE OLD MEN of the Cheyenne over their fires. They whisper the old words.

"A nation is not conquered

until the hearts of its women are on the ground.

Then it is finished,

no matter how brave its warriors

or how strong their weapons."

INTO THE DARK Chief Leg-in-the-Water said, "What do we want to live for? The White Man has taken our country and killed all of our game. He was not satisfied with that, but killed our wives and children."

"Now no peace."

"We want to go and meet our families in the spirit land. We loved the Whites until we found out they lied to us and robbed us of what we had."

"We have raised the battle axe until death."

SEE THE WOMEN wail. See the quick speed of the Cheyenne warriors, an arrow to the heart of the White Man.

III. THE SUICIDE WARRIORS

IN AN AVENGING wildfire the Cheyenne gathered and healed their wounds and rose with vindicated eyes to find and kill White people, and on a day not long after Sand Creek they entered the battle of the Little Bighorn in southeast Montana territory where they took the gold-headed leader of the White men, called Custer, and kissed the earth with his blood.

This they did in a most unassuming way; the lowest and weakest among them gave their lives.

OF THE CHEYENNE, four men. The poorest ones, some young, some old, having no guns, only bow and arrow, club and hatchet, having little and having as yet won little honor. The four made a vow to the people.

"In our next engagement with the White Man, we fight until we die."

Whirlwind, son of Black Crane. Noisy Walking, son of White Bull or Ice. Cut Belly. Closed Hand. The suicide boys of the Cheyenne.

THE DYING DANCE was prepared and when the men entered the circle the people cheered them and celebrated their courage. The men danced all night, the reckless way, painted of white and dark, dancing until morning when they emerged and went out through a camp of eight-thousand Cheyenne, Sioux, and Arapaho, spread four miles along the river.

When they walked, the old men went on either side of them and the criers called out in a loud voice: "Look at these men for the last time. Today they are alive. Today they have thrown their lives away."

THE FOUR joined suicide warriors from the Sioux and together they went with the war party to the field of war. Strategically, they were last to enter the fight, diving on horseback into the enemy's final position. They flew as the spear-point and pierced the enemy. They fought hand to hand and died at gunpoint as the larger mass of warriors flowed in behind, killing Custer and routing his White soldiers, killing them all.

Sitting Bull and Crazy Horse and the combined forces of the Cheyenne, the Lakota Sioux, and the Arapaho orchestrated an advance that left Custer and his two-hundred men dead in less than an hour. A battle of two fronts, one on either side of a winding ridge, the warriors ran the distance between and decimated their enemies.

Over two valleys of dead men, blue sky.

* * *

"HEY JOHN," shouted a man from the balcony, "where'd you get them scalps?"

Chivington mounted the stage at the Appollo Theater in Denver.

"Ladies and gentlemen," he bellowed, big-bodied, feet stamped in a wide stance. In each hand he bore flagpoles. He loved the American flag under the lights, the knot of fifty scalps tied to the tip of each pole, pubic scalps of Cheyenne women atop the mass. He pounded the poles against the stage, the bang like a gunshot, and the people jumped and hooted.

ON THE HIGH PLAINS, after hard mistreatment by the Whites, still Black Kettle sought peace.

BACK AT THE APOLLO. "Though our government did not see fit to reward my accomplishments, I accomplished much. What you see here is the toil of a big man!" On a low table set in front of the audience he displayed the body parts he'd gathered at Sand Creek, some few hands and feet, human fetuses, adult genitalia.

"See here!" he yelled.

"Tell us, John!" cried a fat woman in the front row.

"Gladly," he said, and placed the flagpoles in their dark wood bases. He could hold a crowd. "Just the facts," he said, "I call Indian children nits, you know. Now nits make lice, so I figure we better kill em' all so as to ward off infestation."

The applause was deafening.

When the sound died a large man yelled out, "What about those men of yours, they did some clean work, didn't they?"

"Sure did," he answered. "Carved things up right."

"How'd they do it, John.?"

"Just like you think," he said. "Sat right down on the bodies after we killed em', took out their blades and cut off the parts. Brought em' to town for braggin' rights. See for yourself." He drew his own broadknife and brandished it over the table before him and turned the knife and his head slowly side to side and stared at the faces in the crowd as they whistled and cat-called. Sweat ran from his temples, his head felt red and hot, and he shouted, "Now, listen here!" He moved the knife quick near his neck in a gesture of throat-cutting, and the people grew quiet.

He held still and when there was total silence he said what he wanted:

"Today I declare my unequivocal desire to run for governor of Coloradah!"

The people stood and clapped wildly, hollering their approval.

John Chivington had talked for God and led men, he'd conquered armies and death, but he'd never before felt the surge he felt as the crowd lifted its voice and shouted, full-throated, just for him.

ON A DIFFERENT DAY, some years on, Black Kettle and his wife Woman Here After were pursued heavily, despite Black Kettle's wish for peace even to the end. They were shot and fatally killed as they fell into the water and mud of the Washita River, their bodies pocked with bullets, their bones crushed by the cavalry who rode over them.

LONG DAYS PASSED before Chivington was brought to justice. George Bent, the white interpreter who lived with the Cheyenne the day of the massacre was a half-breed. He was the man married to the Cheyenne woman named Magpie, Black Kettle's cousin. The very man run down by Chivington's horse, the very man who had stood in the way of the charge and raised his hands and pleaded for peace before he screamed, Halt! This man, George Bent, was trampled and lost consciousness, and when he woke with broken ribs, his own innards punctured, he found his wife dead beside him, her body mutilated.

George Bent reported Chivington's deeds and brought Chivington to trial.

Chivington's command was removed, his run for office derailed.

But Chivington lived a long life.

And George Bent died in sorrow, still mourning the death of Magpie.

It was the age of wisdom, it was the age of foolishness...
—Charles Dickens

I have borrowed money.   I have borrowed faith.
—Jorie Graham

THE DEBT MEN

THE DEBT MEN owed all, they owned nothing. Everything borrowed, nothing gained. Everything risked, nothing attained. But in the end, who can say we don't owe even the very breath we take?

Zacharias Harrelson. Phil Silven.

Born into this world.

They were hungry. They were glutted.

Full of life.

Half-dead.

ZACH HARRELSON, angry, borrowed his friend's car until he was arrested on the edge of the Safeway parking lot in north Spokane. He borrowed passed-out Lenny's crystal meth, the keys to the rusted-out Honda along with five dollars, and walked out the door crazed, alive. Five blocks later five policemen put their fists to his face and struck him down like a rabid animal, then beat him on the paved sidewalk at the edge of the parking lot where the people gathered, gawking. The officers rose and holstered their batons, put him in the squad car and drove off, adrenalin like black sand slowing in their pink, translucent veins.

PHIL SILVEN borrowed Italian leather gloves and a white silk scarf from his wife's lingerie drawer.

ZACH Harrelson in dirty t-shirt and jeans without knees, hollow look and hooded eyes, took a tiny loan on a single wide trailer.

PHIL Silven in Versace suit and Gucci watch secured a jumbo loan on a big house on the South Hill ridge so the lights of the city graced the home at night like a sky not above but below and filled with a field of glassy stars.

EVERYONE borrowed, everyone was in debt.

Men not only borrowed for a house, a home. They borrowed for the cathedral of the human heart, the love, the hate, the burden, the fire.

PHIL Silven, determined to remove his wife's germs, borrowed a new pair of his mother's rubber gloves to wear while disinfecting the toilet seat.

ZACH Harrelson borrowed five bucks from the pants pocket of his unconscious friend Len before he borrowed the car. He wanted a box of Hostess raspberry-filled powder donuts from Safeway. He didn't want to walk five blocks, what could be wrong with that? Ten days earlier, his wife had knifed him in the stomach while he slept. He woke to what he recognized as her ugly fat head, skin folds and sweat lines on her neck while the blood pooled on the flat below the arched bones of his ribcage. She stood over him and said calmly, "Take that." He pushed the heel of his hand into the wound and called 911. She took the car and kids and went to Oregon to her mother's house. That was then. Now he wanted donuts. He was lying on the couch with his shirt off, itching the wine-colored threads on the gash above his enflamed bellybutton, the birth knot blue-black and hard as a marble. He still loved her.

PHIL Silven's father, an office manager, fled town with another woman when Phil was 12, leaving the family bankrupt and publicly disgraced (he took ten-thousand dollars from the County Parks and Rec fund). Privately, he had been penetrating Phil for three years, telling the boy he'd kill him if he told. Before he left, Phil took his father's prized stiletto, a possession his father kept in Phil's mother's lingerie drawer— a blade given by Phil's father's father, the Polish-Italian long-haul truck driver ten years dead who had bragged about beating his women. Back then Phil had worn two pairs of tube socks and folded them down to form a thick band over his ankle. He'd slide the black handle of the blade into the slot between his ankle and his achilles where it stayed firm and hidden and he could feel its rigid line and think of grabbing it if he needed to. He'd wore the socks when he slept too, the knife where he liked it. He'd almost felt safe. The weekend his father left, his mother bought him a pair of designer jeans by Armani, Adolfo, and despite his pure hatred for his father, Phil borrowed his father's bravado.

WHEN he was home Zach Harrelson's father slept with a shotgun in his bed. When he wasn't home he slept with the next door neighbor and lied about it and everyone agreed to let him lie even though the neighbor was Helen, Zach's mother's best friend. The night before Zach was knifed in the stomach he brought home three roses from 7-11 for his wife. Zach was hoping to make up for when she caught him high on speed and sexually abusing their six-year-old daughter Jayla. She found him standing over the girl while she slept, his pants down. When his wife walked into the room she slapped him in the back of the head so hard he hit the floor and Jayla woke up crying. Get out, his wife said. No, he said, and rose up and punched her in the chest, then watched as she clutched at her neck like she couldn't breathe.

Roses calm a woman, he thought, help her think straight.

The flowers stooped in a drinking glass on the kitchen counter. Tired of everything, Zach's wife drank a beer and picked out a straight-edged steak knife from the drawer next to the fridge. She heard her husband's breathing, heavy down the hall. It was late afternoon, he was nude, sleeping on top of the bed. She set the beer down on the kitchen table, walked the necessary distance, raised the blade high in her right hand and drove it into the center of his stomach. She took Jayla and left, telling herself she'd never be back. As it went, Zach went to the emergency room, then returned to sit in his house. Ten days passed before he took the bandage off so he could itch the gash more directly. He felt sane when he took his friend's stash, the five bucks, the car. Then he got himself beaten to submission on the edge of the Safeway parking lot. Sitting in County in bright orange coveralls he thought of killing himself.

MEN borrowed desperation, self-degradation.

They borrowed gratitude. They borrowed grace.

45

They desired nothing or desired all, their fate sealed before they were born.

Or fate unfurled, destiny stood before them awaiting the will to ignite.

WHAT men borrowed varied. For one, it was money, another drugs. For one clothes, another swagger. But all, when they were enraged, borrowed the landslide in their father's eyes, and violence entered the blood like a new deficit, ugly, impenetrable, monstrous, increasing.

When Phil Silven returned home at three a.m. on a hot night in July, his wife sat up in bed. Her name was Mary Irene, a weird name for any era, thought Phil. She was full-blooded Hungarian, Irene her great grandmother's name. They had been married five years and had a six-month old daughter, Brianna. Mary Irene watched Phil remove the gloves near the armoire, fold them, kiss them, and place them neatly in his own underwear drawer. She watched him do the same with the white neck scarf. Physically, he was a small man, she a bigger woman; those items were hers once. In a quiet voice she said aloud what she'd been thinking for more than a year. "You're gay." She didn't have time for this. Her boss made her work 60 hours a week. She needed sleep. Phil turned, walked to the bed and slapped her face so hard he left the imprint of his hand like a birthmark on her jaw.

AT THE arraignment Zach Harelson was led into the courtroom and seated in the aisle directly right of where he entered, manacled at the wrists, chained at the ankles. He was the last of fourteen criminals that day. His wife was there, seated in the first row behind the defendants' table, not looking at Zach. Her brother was with her, a fledgling body builder in a tank top and slicked hair, barbed wire tattooed on a black line around both biceps. Zach saw her lips, pursed like wrinkled metal, her eyes like plugs in the flesh of her face. He wanted to abuse her. He sat for two hours. He stood when he was told. A guard walked him to the table and when he passed in front of his wife she rose, spit on the back of his head and said, "Assbag." Her brother pulled her back. The judge told her to sit down.

THE DEBT men borrowed whatever they could, and in the end they borrowed oblivion and rode their debt down until everything collapsed beneath them.

Phil Silven, after slapping his wife, borrowed a bed to sleep on at his friend Paulo's house.

The next weekend Phil Silven undid the knot and took the white silk scarf delicately from around his own neck, handed it to a man with a perfect chest, watched the man shove the scarf quickly, two-handedly into Phil's open mouth and proceeded to be swept into the man's embrace. Fear in Phil's eyes, his heart felt immortal. Hours later at home again he lied straight-faced to his wife. There was no need to borrow anything anymore. It was Saturday night. He had never liked her sex. No, he remembered distinctly, he had liked it a great deal for the first year or two, even loved it. Tonight, she demanded it. No, he decided, he had never liked her sex. She approached and tried to unbutton his jeans. No, he said, but she kept on. He wasn't going to slap her anymore. He put his hands on her and pushed her away. She didn't cry.

"It's someone else," she said.

"Whatever," Phil said.

In the morning over breakfast she berated him. She'd gotten her boss to agree to a two-month extension on her maternity leave but it had ended a month ago and now she was more tired than ever. Their daughter Brianna sat in the high chair. At the end of the argument Mary Irene said, "Admit it, Phil." Then she lifted the plastic table top from Brianna's high chair and threw it at Phil in a swift two-handed motion, bouncing it off the side of his head, making his hair look silly. He watched her pull Brianna from the chair and clutch her to her chest. His wife's face was blotchy. He rose and approached and tore the child from her arms. He left the house and took Brianna to Mass at Our Lady Fatima. When he returned home his wife was seated with her hands face down on the kitchen table.

"I want a divorce," she said.

"Fine," he said.

She got the child.

He got the house.

MEN grew progressively more ugly, fulfilling want by whatever means necessary.

But on the other side some emerged, broken, and better.

Days bled into night and night became day and all became one, and all men did not stagnate. Yes, some remained the same. But some became more vital.

ZACH served his debt to society and when he walked from the cement and metal structure in the middle of town his wife got out of her car and greeted him sheepishly and took him into her arms saying, "My Baby, Baby, good Baby. It's okay now, Baby. Good Baby Boy." He held her face in his hands and kissed her long and hard and with his tongue.

TWENTY years on, Phil Silven, twenty years divorced from Irene, sat with her at a table in the back of a room in a hall lit by chandeliers. On the dance floor, their daughter danced with her partner Lee Anne, army pilot who flew Blackhawks. The wedding was exquisite.

Mary Irene held Phil's hand. "I was hard on you," she said.

He looked at her. "And I you," he said.

"You're happy with Paulo. I can see that."

"Thank you."

"Our daughter," she said, looking out.

"Yes," he said. "Our daughter."

"Thank you," she said.

He leaned in and took Mary Irene's face in his hands and kissed her forehead gently, with the love we knew when we began, alone and alive in this world.

—for my cousin Jacine who died young, because of violent men

THE CURRENT KINGS

TO THE BROTHER'S bedroom, sleep-deprived, half-dead, seeking a high from which they might not descend, they find what they envision and pump the body electric. Full, filled, and running over, replete, sensorial, ravenous, unquenched, unkempt and empty-eyed out the front door, walking far and manic to the parkade at Sacred Heart. Both have guns, right front pocket of puffed up coats—.357 Magnum and a .44— and each has in the heart as physical and vocal as the weapons they carry the indent of his father-loss and mother-hunger, his manner of dominating others, annihilating self, withering, wallowing, bellowing. Self, silo, solipsism, system, can't put a finger on whose fault it is.

They move fluid as water along dim-lit walls of corrugated steel seeking someone unaware with whom to make a more vibrant transaction, anxious and amped, not afraid but full of fear, and fear-inducing, fear-invoking—and people spread from them as ripples from a thrown stone, barely acknowledging, yet noticing, intently, the gravity. Women hustle children into cars, men look up angrily but drive swiftly away, and when in aggravation they verbally accost first a young male accountant as he fumbles keys to ignition, and second a middle-aged female hospital executive—the parking authority is informed and the two are summarily dismissed from the premises.

Out along 3rd Street down among the city heat, stoplights, homeless, nicotine, gasoline, to the central bus station and vivid images of the human skull and hand, the mouth yelling, and their two forms moving into an alcove at the base of a second parkade, ancillary to American Savings and Trust, in like reptiles herking, jerking up stairs, labyrinthine bodies, hand to the gun shaft, slamming outward into the paved overearth, rebar-ceilinged open air where they come abruptly upon a fat man bloat-faced guard whose presence makes them discretely withdraw their guns to silent cover, and whose words, vitriolic, full of bile, hateful, powerful, pernicious, send them reeling back down the stairwell and out into the street again where they walk downhill and further north to the river, embittered as they go, vowing under cover of dusk and coming dark to find and kill and assuage the shame, hearken to the pull of the anguish that reaches and holds their hands, warm, hard, metallic inside their coats.

Over the bridge, spitting on cars, they spill into the next parking lot. Slab of asphalt vast and dark on the land side of the River Hotel and Conference Center, the two-tower building a contemporary battlement over the river. They look up and see a marquee in the sky:

Welcome National Convention

LATE AFTERNOON near dark the world dims in the east and the vault overhead appears bruised. Clouds on the western line sit like columned fires and among them the sun burns red and big as a bowl. The shadow of Blacksburg lengthens on the earth-curve. The boys have never been there.

A woman walks from her car at the lot edge out into a span of asphalt free of other vehicles. A woman unknown to them on a line to the blazing glass of the conference center where the sun's glare makes a perfectly luminous wall connected in massive congruity to a host of small rectangles above it, each individual room, each open-eyed inferno witness to the world. The boys approach quickly and shove the guns to her head bumping the skull bone, rushing her back to her car. They snatch her keys and push her into the backseat where one follows and sits above and over her while the other drives, laughing at her and themselves while she, 25 and engaged to be married, prays for them and thinks clearly, gun to head, what she might say to show and give love, not hold on, not cower, not falter.

"God is light," she says, trying to look into their faces, "and in him is no darkness."

"Shut up," they say, marveling at how the barrel of the gun bumps her head forcing her face down and away.

"Please," she says. "Don't."

"Don't what?" the boy in the back snaps.

"Don't do what you are doing."

"Shut up," he says.

Her mouth is dry, her hands wet.

"Don't look at me," he says.

She looks down, whispering, "You don't need to do this."

"Do what? Shut up! Put your head down!" He pushes the pipe of the gun at the corner of her forehead, knocking on the bone. He taps her forehead twice. Three times. Smiles. Laughs.

"No," she says, her voice as hard and foreign to her as an animal's. Hearing it, she lifts her head, opens her arms and sets her hands on her thighs.

"Stay down," he says, tapping her skull with the gun again.

She doesn't respond. "Come back with me to the conference," she says. Her voice is clear and vivid. "We can go back and get help. We don't have to say anything. We don't have to involve the police. We can get out of this."

"Count to ten," the boy driving says, eyeing the road. "I can't drive like this."

"Can't drive period, rathead," the other answers. "Besides, talk all she wants. Won't matter. I'm putting her out."

"10," he says.

"Wait," she puts her hands up in front of her face, shaking. "9."

"Listen." She begins singing and the count stops. Tin grind of road and thin tires. Smell of heat and fear, sweat, her upper lip slick, and over everything her words like leaves falling.

"Is there any forgiveness for the things I've done..." She looks into his eyes.

"Is there pardon for sinners, I know that I'm one..."

"What's this," he says, and smiles, and to her surprise, he listens. Finger set to the trigger, he rests the gun in his lap and listens, he gives her this, and considers her.

"Will you take this heart of foulness... and make it clean again? Will you pour on me your mercy... if I confess my sin...

"8," he says. He looks out the window, beyond her.

"Oh Lord forgive me." Her voice cries out.

"7."

"I need your mercy."

"6."

"I need your..."

"5."

She moves her head nearer and looks at him. They turn a curve and his face burns, struck gold by sun. His eyes half-closed, she puts her hand on his arm. He jerks his arm away. "I want you to know," she says.

"4," he says, staring at her.

"I know you. You and me. We're one."

"3."

"I know you are going to kill me."

"2."

"And I forgive you."

"1."

STROKE OF THUNDER from the barrel, concussive blow and loud bang in the air, white fire leaping through bone, velocity piercing seat and wheel-well so the back right end of the vehicle slams down, tire shot through, and red in the chamber, and red on the rim, and red that begins and never ends. Three more in quick succession: bang, bang, bang. A pause. Two more: bang, bang.

Her body on this side of the divide, silent.

The boys giggling, spitting, screaming. "Go! Go! Go!"

But the car has become fatal and won't drive, and so they let it die at the shoulder and as the sun goes out they flee the metal box, down the reedy descent to the floodwall of the river to where they run among rocks and trees for two miles back to the glow of the lights and the fierce contraction of dark and dawn until they emerge finally at the lip of the Market Street Bridge and walk like kings into the city.

"Walter," she said, looking full upon him with her affectionate eyes, "like you, I hope for better things. I will pray for them, and believe that they will arrive."

—Charles Dickens

BEFORE HE SLEEPS

HE CAN'T SEE where she's gone and he can't hear her. He doesn't wait either, his footsteps heavy, thin body down the hall, long-boned feet and outbent legs, knees like tight fists in the dark pull of his clothing. She is eighty-one. He is eighty-five. He was big once. He is nothing now. Above his body, the hard odd-shaped sphere of his skull, his neck is too slender, and he pauses, finds his face in the oval mirror as he opens the front door. Narrow hall that houses him, walls eggshell white.

He leaves these walls behind.

Stay or go? In the static of dreams, he can never seem to answer rightly.

He'll have to walk fast, he tells himself, forget how she drew blood from his face, the bridge of his nose, the half-circle of bone below his eye if his memory still serves him. She wakes in the bed beside him, lifts her torso over his. She places her hands on his shoulders, peers at him in the dark while he sleeps, and he thinks she might take her piece of flesh again. He'll watch himself wake. He'll hold her wrists like chicken bones. Tears from the crease of her eyes, catlike hiss in the flat triangle of her mouth, he comes back to himself and folds her forearms in over her and presses her bodily into his chest holding her until the strangeness falls away and he feels her body resolve and she breathes and she sleeps. Fine feel of her frame over the shell of him, he turns and lays her down. She'll sleep for a long time now, he thinks.

"The nurse is stealing my shoes."

He imagines she'll say this when she wakes. Small slippers, soft and pink, he'll show her these at the foot of the bed, the same slippers he tries to remember her wearing, walking down the two lanes of West Park Street among the big metal cars, crying. The way he sees it, it was her. Not him in his old man house shoes, plaid and flat-soled, archless, him having fallen and bruised his forehead, his hands, his heels. She sees him in the street, slowly getting up again, cars like insects swarming as he walks. He is like a drunk, he knows it, but also not, not like someone sleep can redeem. Lost, he thinks, inexorably, as the world slips away. No longer able anymore to find who or where he is. He rubs the old wounds, still fresh, the open scabs on his hands, the frontal bone of his head sore as if struck by pipe or stone. He curses at cars. I hope no one else finds her, he thinks, before I come to carry her home. *You are the Devil, I rebuke you.* The thoughts ruin his mind if he heeds them.

Late afternoon sun, late autumn Livingston, Montana, September, leaves like paper dolls taped to the fingers of trees, red-gold, full of light. The silver spine of the Crazy Mountains out far on the arc of the world. He believes he holds her bird body in his arms, walking, and that she will spit in his face, her jaw shaking before he sits her down at the kitchen table for rye bread, tea, and jam. *What did I do to you?* he thinks. *How have I failed you?* Her lips move, but he hears no voice. His face falls. "I have failed you," he whispers. He walks the yellow mid-line in a flow of traffic, mumbling, "She suffered when I lost him. Our boy not yet 20. Car wreck that let me be, even as he died." The man won't pronounce the name. He doesn't want to remember.

After today, he believes he won't have to take care. He'll be gone. He'll leave her alone. Her stale bedclothes and tangled hair, her black colostomy bag and the face she gives when he cleans her—he'll be sorry to be rid of these small acts of contrition, but relieved too, he grimaces, like the shuffle of new feet in the street. He raises his arms, walking the yellow lines, forgetting the noise that blares, the big voices and honking horns. He was a superhuman fatalist in depression, he remembers, and she had cried and laid her head on his back, whether he wished for it or not. After the funeral he had placed himself face down on the floor in the basement and wouldn't come out. He'd thought then of his shoulder blades inverted like steel shovels pushed down through his chest, digging into the dirt beneath him. She had come to *him* then, and he was only forty, forty-three, and she'd rubbed his feet and listened to him breathe, and when she called he responded as she hoped he would, her feminine mouth inviting him to come up and eat dinner with her. A man will hear the kind words of his wife. Gone, now, walking. His breath is sour. His feet at odds with the road. He'll take the bus when he gets to it. He likes the sun. He hates how people scream in his ear. He's convinced he doesn't care what she thinks. She's lost her slippers and she'll never find them. I won't help her and she'll cry and lose her mind and I won't care. When I'm gone there will be no one to find her and bring her back. No one to catch her when she falls. Not me. Not anyone. He'll put his neck on the vinyl headrest of a Greyhound, outbound, all the way west, Puget Sound, electric wires set on the nerve endings of his exposed teeth.

Nothing feels right as he watches his feet. They are big and slow and they aim his face too far forward and he trips, bludgeoning his own head. His mind is thick. He is older than he wants to be, a fool splayed in the street in dirty pale pajamas, thin red pinstripes, people yelling, "Out of the way!" "Get up, old man!"

He curses himself. He curses them, "Shut your rotten caves!"

I'm helpless, he thinks, though a moment earlier he was convinced it was him helping her, not her who must find and secure him and draw him back to where he is meant to be. He is in bed. He has gone nowhere. Here. Not there. Me. Not her. Me, he concludes. And he is convinced, his mind having slipped and gone, and returned again, that she was never gone.

In bed, he turns to her.

"Quiet," she says.

She leans her body over him. Takes his hand. Forms his fingers to cup her face.

"Here," she says, "I'm here."

The knife is like a point of light or heat. The flash of blade a sun-white orb, dime-sized, shining on the skin under his jaw. His eyes are wide, the house cavernous, his dry whisper, whispering back, "No."

"Yes," she says.

She'll use the weapon, he thinks, dumb gift he'd thought her not nimble enough to notice, the letter opener from his retirement party, IH on the handle, the truck company that employed him for most of his life:

INTERNATIONAL HARVESTER

Point of malice, he thinks. She touches him under the bones of his mouth, beneath his mandible, skin folds, fallen. She stares, her body clamped over his rigid frame. Her right fist is destiny, he thinks, and he feels her shove herself forward over him, blade through the underside of the jaw and upward, easy as he imagined, through the roof of the mouth and up through the face plate and orbital bone, all the way to the wet socket of the eye.

Yes, he thinks she does these things, but what he thinks and what he receives do not converge. He feels no pain. He breathes easy. It is her common hands that hold him, his face and dying eyes, and this he remembers, her touch on his forehead, the light of her face like twilight, delicate mouth and light breath.

This, he remembers before he sleeps.

FIRE

Concealed sorrow bursts the heart, and rages within us as an internal fire.

—Ovid

Whoever the murderer is, I know him: not his identity, but his coming about, in this time and place.

—Eudora Welty

THE DIPLOMAT

THE AIR he breathed was filled with the acidic tailings of anti-artillery guns and a punk smell that issued from the mouths of rebel rocket launchers. On the courtyard's perimeter, eight-foot thick fortified concrete encompassed the compound, built six months back just after the previous regime fell. Two light attack tanks with short-range missile capacity were posted at the gates, steel boxes of malice with a select few Marines who would soon leave this place. Two women, three men, so trim in their uniforms, and with such clean faces. Unbearably young, he thought. They called him Government 14, or the Specialist, or the Diplomat. He liked the sound as it rolled from their mouths. The other Westerners were nearly all gone. He especially liked being called the Diplomat.

He wasn't all the way down. He still kept up with events back home, but not the way others did. In his old age he was drawn to the shadow of atrocity, seeking to understand his country's racism to see what it might yield, America still ravenous, he thought, still so stubbornly self-embedded. Back home, silencing accompanied bodily harm. He couldn't escape that fact and didn't want to anymore. Misogyny laced with misandry, the old warring with orientation, intimacy, and alienation. In his own life he'd borne both pity and shame, not a small portion warranted, alongside that which he thought unwarranted, but in the end when he tallied the ledger he felt the sum of his accomplishments amounted to very little. He was stationed nowhere now, in a country of woe. In fact, until he'd met the young man, he wasn't sure if he wanted out at all. He'd thought he might just die here in decline. But with the young foreigner a rebirth had come and the fortifications he'd made in his mind, of despair, of his own disregard, were weaker now.

Should I be given the grace, he thought, I'll leave here. I'll live again.

THE MEETING had occurred when he walked down an alley to retrieve the car after dinner, the city then undestroyed. A chance meeting: the young man aslant in the back door of a poorly-made apartment, the slight upper body, the draw of the neck to the jaw line. Pale yellow shirt. Look of want in his eyes. As for what gave the boy confidence the Diplomat credited his own regal bearing in his blue suit, his ebony cufflinks imprinted like black tacks at his wrists, his red tie emblazoned with gold.

The boy stared into the Diplomat's face.

"Do you need money?" the Diplomat asked.

"No," he answered.

"What then?"

"Guns." The young man said. "Safety."

He looked at the young man's arms. He assured himself this was only the economies of man to man. But he let himself gaze into the boy's eyes, dark and open discs, and when the boy reached and placed a hand on his he thought suddenly of fires that consumed everything whole. A feeling entered him like the dislodge of earth that precedes a landslide.

"Please help," the boy said. "Help us. They killed my mother and father. My sisters." He could not have been 18 years old. The Diplomat released him. A moisture to the skin, he thought, like the leaves outside the office window at the embassy. In the stairwell another man appeared, slightly older, backlit and standing as if lost, shirtless, a chest and face that captured light and shone like something otherworldly.

"Are you in danger?" the Diplomat asked.

From a lightbulb on the near wall shadows made angles of their faces.

"We are not like them," the boy motioned with his chin, toward the city. "They hurt us. They want us dead." His eyes looked hollow. The boy motioned to the older one behind him. "Us," he said. The first boy took a step forward. "They tied my father to a post." He looked over the Diplomat's shoulder.

The Diplomat wavered.

If it was just the young one perhaps, without the other.

He had come to this country to avoid entanglement. He took out his wallet and placed money in the boy's hand. The boy took it and reached, clutching the hem of his suit coat. "Stay," the boy said, "We'll cook poulet bicyclette. Or you want mafé? Or kedjenou? We'll cook for you." The boy looked back again, his lips straight as the edge of an envelope. He waved the Diplomat in but the Diplomat stepped away. He disliked mafé. He loved bicyclette and the spicy stew of kedjenou. Anything with guinea fowl. Anything without peanuts.

"I'll come find you," the Diplomat said. Or I won't, he thought.

But driving he watched the rearview mirror, the boy's face a blown fuse.

A MONTH passed, two.

The fighting intensified in the north.

He wanted to keep an eye on the boy and started visiting the area near the apartment on "official" business. Nearly always he saw nothing. Twice though, he witnessed him from a distance and each time the Diplomat felt hard-chested, as if hit by something that would level him to the ground. But as the days drew on he saw the boy only once more, a fleeting glimpse of the pale yellow polo as the boy rounded a corner.

A YEAR from the first meeting the Diplomat still thought of him.

From his office window he stared through the branches of an olive tree. He made out the barricade erected against the front gate beyond the tanks. The sun, incandescent at the edge of the world appeared to weep in the smoke that lingered toward evening. Like small candles, fires burned in the far reaches of the city.

Next to the window a map of the continent covered one wall, the outline rugged, the surface various shades of brown for each country, the boundary lines old and redrawn in red ink to chart the new world. The land mass in the shape of a prehistoric axe, he thought. Huge. Malformed. The country he knew now was the southern cut of the blade, bloody Liberia to the west, and to the east Ghana, Togo, Benin. Nigeria as big as an ox. Throughout, the violent kiss of Islam and Christianity. The largest stretch of the handle held Cameroon, the Congo, Angola, and Namibia, all the way to the bottom of the hilt where South Africa stood freighted with vengeance and atonement. The millions of deaths from the cape to the curve of the country were unfathomable.

This country. His own Thermopylae.

The people need me, he thought. No, he countered, no one needs anyone.

He'd selected the post some years back when the country appeared calm. His first choice. A site of ease and relative comfort for the years before retirement. But when the embassy was moved from upcountry to the south he could only nod his assent. The U.S. Diplomatic Corps chose a pillared two-story French Colonial with acutely-peaked gables. The building stood a mile south of the city center, in a clutch of upper middle-class housing that bled to poverty a few streets further on.

The war had followed him here.

His office was housed on the second floor of a small beleaguered fortress.

Spanish military airplanes had evacuated foreign civilians from Admiral H Airport, and French expats had needed to be lifted from the roofs of their houses to escape the mobs. Until recently, he and the rest of the Americans were largely ignored. Then the worst of it came, the soldiers taking him to identify the body of a male co-worker whose face he barely recognized. The head was decapitated and set beside the body. Open eyes. Dirty teeth. The body had been dragged through the streets, the wound at the neckline something unforeseen and terrible. He retched, soiling his shirt before the soldiers led him back to the tank and returned him to the embassy.

After witnessing the body, he knew he needed to act. By agreement with rebel forces he'd arranged a U.N. escort to see the last staff member off at the depot ten miles beyond the northern edge of the city. His hands wouldn't stop shaking when he stood watching the narrow cars shift west around one broad corner out into an open field, the train monolithic with its layered spine that hinged and absorbed the turn and carried the vessel onward. He felt afraid for himself. He focused his line of vision on the blue hats of the U.N. soldiers. Beyond them he saw the severe face of his assistant, Marie from Oklahoma, framed by a thin glass window over steel wheels on black rails. A stench of tarred wood and oil. She had not imagined this, he thought, her body, her person abhorred in the heart of the continent. In the last days her fear had gained total control, the lines of her face creasing to a new depth.

He watched the tight brown bowl of her hair disappear north.

In his office, his impotence burdened him now. Even before the beheading almost everyone accused him of irreversible failures. His wife who divorced him long ago. Girlfriends. Boyfriends. His own children. And now in this place as in every place previous, those who worked for him respected him little and uttered the same tired message: *he does nothing, he's inept.* And it was true; he'd proved himself incapable of generating the international good will the position demanded. The reputation of his own country's bully government had not helped. The work was intractable.

Still, his charges were safe, weren't they?

He needed to help himself now.

He pictured them on the train. Their nervous laughter. An exhalation in the shoulders as they crossed the border. Your body still breathing is not nothing, he thought.

He stared out the window over his desk. Out far, the city burned.

He would need to be on the next U.N. helicopter.

I won't make it out alive, he thought.

In the courtyard below, a white flamingo tilted on one leg between the two light attack tanks. The Marine soldiers were seated bold-faced atop the tanks. A faint strain of anxiety in the lean of their bodies. The bird's wings opened for a moment before the creature craned its neck, coiled inward and tucked a black-tipped beak between the body and the fold of a wing. The head of the bird utterly serene.

In the distance, great fires.

THE NEXT DAY the Diplomat did the unthinkable. He ran to the front gate and scrambled over the barricade. The soldiers shouted at him but he disappeared into the labyrinth of streets and ran for some minutes before he slipped behind a brick wall. He wore dark clothing and a hooded top, a black bandana over his mouth and chin. His breath came heavy. He ran again until he saw the Basilica on his right, the white domed cathedral with a high columned portico and breezeways that armed outward from the central edifice. Our Lady of Hope, a miracle of marble carved from the jungle. City of excess, veined with abject need. Depravity and sacredness, he told himself, and looked at the backs of his hands.

He walked at a brisk pace past the high bulb of the radio beacon and thought of the people and their faith, their enigmatic evidence of things unseen. He passed the square towers of the mosque where gold domes painted arabesques on the sky and made his way north along the water where he searched near the restaurant.

He went to the alley and found nothing.

Night fell. He wandered and finally walked back to the water, down to the lagoon that encased the city center and underlined a cityscape that was a low progression of greater and lesser buildings. The urban enclave was built solely for the legacy of Admiral H. Built by Admiral H himself. From above, the water opened like the mouth of a lion, the lagoon's wide jaws the northern end of a U-shaped passage that was the final stop before the living arrangements grew impoverished again and the city became a township dense with tin.

Called the Meadow of the Old World, Admiral H had built a wildlife enclosure on the banks of the lagoon where the only animals left were a tribe of olive baboons whose gray-green faces held elongated jaws and housed tall, fearsome teeth. Also known as Anubis baboons after the Egyptian dog-faced god, their shoulders were like cannonballs, their muscled torsos and long arms hunched over hardened haunches. They set their fists like mallets on the ground.

All was quiet now.

For a great while the Diplomat watched the water and searched the banks. He wondered how many of them moved in the dark below. He decided finally to return to the embassy, but as he moved a short distance off into the streets he heard an uproar and when he rounded a sharp corner he encountered people rushing forward. Their chaotic feet stomped the ground as they ran. Pretending nonchalance, he entered the flow. He thought with strain of his pale face and hands. His neck like a column of alabaster. He shrouded himself in his hood and tucked his hands under his arms. Yelling issued from makeshift bullhorns. Slogans of venom and death on the air. The bright darkness of faces and rough lines of bodies bobbing and tilting. He took a diagonal through the crowd but a few steps in he was cross-grain and immovable. Keeping his head down, he tried to shoulder himself forward but the crowd tightened. The people toted wooden clubs, shafts of pipe, belts, bottles. The weapons were primitive, the violence ancient, and as he pulled his hood fully over his face he lost balance and fell. He felt a tremendous blow to the stomach from a blunt object, a knee perhaps, or the head of a baseball bat. The crowd trampled him in the dark. He lost breath and for a moment consciousness.

When the night appeared again above him, the crowd was gone. A dog with the face of a jackal approached tentatively and licked his face.

The mob had passed north into the city.

He limped away in the darkness, south.

AT THE GATE he shouted warning and made his way again over the barricade. A black sergeant from Seattle, one of the Marines, shone a bright light on him, eyed him sideways and shook his head. "Dumb as hell," the sergeant muttered.

"What?" the Diplomat said, pausing. He approached the sergeant, too close, his face a hand-width from the man's nose. A narrow nose, the Diplomat thought, with a square bridge.

"Back up," the sergeant said, pressing his hand on the Diplomat's chest.

The touch set the Diplomat back some, but he pushed forward anyway. "I'll back up whenever I damn well please," he said.

"You'll back up when I say back up," the sergeant said, thumping the Diplomat's sternum with his fist.

The knuckles hurt him, and he receded. "I need..." he said, moving away.

"You need?" the sergeant called.

"Nothing," the Diplomat mumbled.

He held his side as he entered the front door. Limping, he ascended the stairs and crossed the threshold into his office where he stood and gazed out the window at the outline of the olive tree before he sat down at his desk, leaned back in the wooden swivel chair and closed his eyes.

His life had been about infrastructure: Ecuador first and El Salvador, and now thirty years on the dark continent, the bad years in the midlands, stints in the west, the east during peace, and far north where a stone's throw over water, the middle east was in uproar. He'd done little, he reminded himself. But since he met the young man his view of the future had changed. Whenever he thought of the boy, the collarbones and eyes, the voice filled of what the Diplomat took to be affection— everything spoke to him of what he'd not known for a great while. What he had in fact diminished or denied. Perhaps destroyed. He put his face in his hands. He wanted love.

The words returned to him in his ex-wife's voice: *You wrecked this family.* The Diplomat had two kids, a girl he'd never attended to and a boy he tried to forget, and there was his ex, alive somewhere, hating him with a deadly hatred. And why not? he admitted. He'd burned every bridge. His parents had been Roman Catholic. For a time, in his first year at Georgetown, he'd thought he might become a Jesuit. He didn't know what he was now. Twenty years ago it came like a flood, his wife's discovery of his women and men and porn and massage parlors and whores. She'd released him like dead weight. On furlough they'd taken the ferry north from Prince Rupert to Alaska where she and the kids would stay with her parents. On the point above the old WWII gun batteries in Sitka, the ocean stone-grey to the horizon, she told him she'd be happy when he was dead. Her face an anvil in the dark. She took everything, including his coal black lab, Foucault.

He no longer felt anything about it. His life, he thought, was one of deep and abiding failures.

He told himself not to go out again. Did he want to die?

Strangely, he thought, he wanted to live more than ever now.

But the city had fulminated to an ungodly harvest. And where was the boy? The boy had begged him. "Help me. Help us." The Diplomat imagined the mob hovering like predators over the boy. The strong devour the weak. An unending pendulum of gouged eyes and duct-taped mouths, torn bodies and machete-hacked limbs. Hangings. Blame it on the French, he thought, or the people themselves. He considered his own hypocrisy. The blood mark of America could never be removed. Her decadence. Her privilege and dominance, how she worshipped her white skin. Closer still, his children had been completely unearthed by him. Torn out by the roots. He wanted to explain to them all, this wasn't who he was. He was something more.

He folded his arms and put his head down on the desk, breathing slowly, in and out. The writings of Carl Jung came to him, from readings early in his career when he'd devoted himself solely to the man's work. His days had felt full then, nearly infinite and at the same time infinitesimal. *The less embodied the shadow, the darker and denser it is.* The less spoken, he thought. The American machine—hyper-capitalist, supremacist—could not speak of its own shadow but in archaic half-truths that meant erasure. Being gay primarily, he too had been erased by it, and yet I am part and parcel, he thought. Borne aloft by history. His pale skin and dark eyes. He didn't know what to do with the knowledge. In white America the shadow was disembodied. Women-hating and contempt for men, he thought, he was progenitor of the hatred to come, both its heir and conduit. Men eroticized hatred not only for women but also for the butch, the femme, the bottom. He only wanted communion, he thought, abandon in the body of another.

He'd followed the outlets that spoke of white-sponsored terror in the U.S., and what to do in the aftermath, of which no one seemed to have an answer. Charleston, Jacksonville,

72

Beavercreek, Ferguson, Sanford, Staten Island, L.A., Rodney King, Eric Garner, Trayvon Martin, Michael Brown, John Crawford, Jordan Russel Davis, the beautiful Reverend Honorable Clementa Pinckney and beloved Mother Emanuel. Back through all existence a white line of torture—slavery, rape, lynching, murder. Whole families hung from the Mississippi bridge as late as the 1950s. Being born in Montana, when he applied for the Diplomatic Corps he'd researched the atrocities against the Blackfeet on the Marias, the Nez Perce at the Big Hole, and the massacre at Sand Creek where U.S. Calvary dismembered Cheyenne elders, women and children, parading the body parts on the Apollo Stage in Denver, the pubic scalps of women, human fetuses.

Whenever he reckoned America, he felt self-hatred.

Raising his head, he saw the inferno.

Flames had spread now over the city, metastasizing from a localized to a global wound—we can't move on, he thought, we won't be allowed to. Who can atone? He remembered Claudia Rankine:

"Citizen. A measure of all memory is breath. To breathe you have to create."

Create dangerously. As Camus created.

He pushed thumb and forefinger to his side, grimacing. Through connections at three embassies, he'd bribed and falsified in order to find a route through Morocco to Spain, to Great Britain, and finally D.C. He'd succeeded in gaining two berths, and now when he stared at the papers set before him on the desk, the boy seemed to him a kind of new destiny. A U.N. helicopter would be too obvious. The boy would accompany him by train. Discretion the heart of diplomacy, he would take the boy in secret. He folded the papers in a white business envelope and locked them in his desk.

THE NEXT DAY he entered the city again.

Heavy fighting in the southwest. From the back porch he crossed the grass and climbed the embassy wall with a rope he looped over one of the metal stanchions. From the corner of the house the sergeant stood watching. The Diplomat ignored him. At the top the Diplomat flipped the rope free and traversed the eight-foot wide surface and made his descent on the other side. He hid the rope in the brush and moved into the streets where he walked fast.

He hoped the boy was not bruised, or worse, dead.

The air stunk of smoke and oil, gasoline and the heat of unnatural fires. Technicals and roving trucks, open-backed and filled with rebel soldiers, roamed the streets. He hid in alcoves and entryways, pressed his face to windows and peered in. He tried to calm his breathing. The drone of the vehicles receded. He entered the city center and came again to the alley, where he found the door, the building structurally unsound now with sections of roof torn away and open caverns on the second floor.

He knocked. No one answered.

He knelt and placed his hands on the door.

He rose and walked a block further on.

There is nothing for me now, he thought.

Like a vagrant, he sat down where the dirt of the street met the crumbled archway of what had been a stone house. He never knew his father, a scientist, an engineer at Los Alamos. His mother was made of needles. Below severity, fear, he thought. Below belief, intimacy. He stared out for what seemed to him a very long time.

Returning to the embassy after sundown, he secured the rope and climbed and lay down on his back atop the wall. His limbs felt heavy. He stared at the night overhead, a blackness dense and starless, and thought of the succulents of the lower Karoo desert at the southern tip of the continent, plants obscure and hardly visible until the rains came and they blazed to life. Red and yellow blooms open-mouthed like a shout. When they died they were quick to die. A sweet aroma remained. Atop the wall, the scent came to him, airy and high like good Riesling. In his weariness his eyes stung. He admitted here in this country of famine with the city's infrastructure pounded to oblivion his thoughts were not for his own survival, though he still held some little hope. What did the French say? *Sans* ego. Complete abandon, he thought. Oceans and continents from any semblance of family, a simple fact came to his awareness: love is not lonely. Love, the reality to which he'd always been wed in the ache of his own self-imposed unreality.

The reality of love appeared to him now as if written in fire, of a love he felt would never be realized.

Feeling sorry for himself, he thought it was a gift just to have met the boy.

Stay stoic, he told himself, stay alive, and he rose, descended the wall, and returned to his office.

IN THE MORNING when he woke on the office floor, there was silence over the land. He lay on his side, and when he heard the roar of attack planes strafing the city, the whine of bombs dropped from the sky, still he didn't move. He stared sideways at the room and noticed a decanter of five-hundred dollar cognac on the glass surface atop a grey elephant's foot. Five lead crystal tumblers. The rest of the liquor would be wasted. He rose to his knees, filled the tumblers and sat on the floor with his back to the wall. He took the first glass to his lips and threw it back, the liquid like a hot coal in his throat. He set the glass on the floor beside him and took the second glass and tipped it back in a leisurely way, the burn less pronounced, as if he'd swallowed a thorn. He put the empty glass on the floor beside the first and sat still and rested his hands on his thighs. He recalled the words of his wife at night early in the marriage when he woke to find her quietly weeping next to him.

"What is it?" he'd asked.

Her answer upended him.

"I am afraid to own a body," she said. "I am afraid to own a soul."

He had held her then until she slept.

Now his heart felt weary. When he first came to the city they led him to the Palace of the Admiral where he stood in a crowd of tourists and witnessed live chickens fed to the baboons. A racket of wing and panic. The snap of jaws followed by the crunch of bone. Spattered blood. A push of adrenaline. With their hands the baboons tore the birds open. He'd been more enthralled than he wanted to admit. Thinking of the boy now, his mind tipped over. He put his head back to the wall and pressed the heels of his hands to the corners of his eyes. He wanted to consume. He wanted to be consumed. What could be wrong with desire? The boy would want for nothing. He downed another glass and his eyes swam, no blade to the liquor any longer, just a bend that moved him lower down the wall so he rested his chin on his chest and he seemed to watch his thoughts swirl and break apart. The boy would leave his lover. For the boy's own safety the older one would let him leave. The Diplomat double-fisted the last two glasses and when his head went hard he heard the bump and bounce of the tumblers on the floor. His body fell over and he felt a sharp tap on the upper left side of his skull.

DAY CYCLED to night and when the sun shone again he woke to a pronounced throb at the corner of his forehead. He touched at the upraised button of skin there. The bone felt bruised. He sat up and went to the bathroom where he washed his face and smoothed his hair. The redness at his hairline looked angry. He took a shower and changed his clothes. He went to his desk and held one hand to his side, the other to his head. He perused the list he'd made, meaningless now in the state of things, but a comfort to him: water, money, passport, evacuation orders. The great booming in the west was closer now. His insides ached. He had not thought of the dread of death in quite this way before. No train. He would forgo the boy. He needed to make the phone call for an escort by helicopter east and then north skirting Burkina Faso. A car ride from there to Morocco. A long ride. He lifted the receiver and listened to the dial tone.

Dispatch expects me, he thought.

He looked over the courtyard.

The soldiers were gone.

He hung up the phone.

He walked out the front door and over the barricade into the city where he pretended he was sane though the streets were filled with riot and there was great danger in wearing what he wore. The suit and tie. His own skin. Now his death would be terrible, he thought. As he walked, his inner thighs began to rub and his heart palpitated. The envelope was in the inner chest pocket of his suit, concealing money wrapped in wax paper and further wrapped in the two documents he'd obtained. His signature was there, yes, but more crucial was the signature of the region chief whose demarcation covered the entire span of the continent from here to North Africa. He passed over and down to where the baboons fed, and in the light of dusk he saw the aftermath of the feedings, a track of blood and

77

feathers in a wine-colored swath from the landing to the stairs of the palace. From there he turned and crossed back into the city's core where he walked the road to the restaurant and through the alley. Again the boy was nowhere to be found and the Diplomat's heart dropped and he said aloud, "Never mind."

Turning, he entered an empty jewelry store, a place half-collapsed and badly burned. He felt forsaken but when he turned again, the boy appeared in the doorjamb of the building across the street. The Diplomat faced him directly. The young man seemed unfamiliar, his blank face touched with more disaffection than the Diplomat remembered. Then the boy's eyes softened. Sleek head and sleek body. He wanted to hold the boy to his chest and watch the boy fall asleep. I fade, but he remains, the Diplomat thought.

The boy nodded.

His aquiline nose, his lips and narrow face, the cheekbones and infinitely the eyes.

He is too third world, the diplomat told himself. Pins for legs, eyes more yellow than white, a concave torso like a cavity in the earth. Why am I here? he wondered. The old questions of border and boundary: *Who are you? Where are you going? What do you have to declare?*

He stepped forward, crossed the street and touched the boy's shoulder.

Love is the vessel we ferry between us, the Diplomat thought.

He opened his suit coat and moved his lips but no words came.

The boy stared, then rotated slightly and looked over his shoulder into the stairwell.

"Do you need my help?" the Diplomat asked.

Facing the Diplomat again, the boy drew a pistol from the small of his back and pointed it at the Diplomat's chest.

"Shut up," the boy said.

The boy stepped forward, touching the gun to the top of the Diplomat's head. The Diplomat rocked on his heels. He felt split in two. "Be still!" the boy said. "Put your head down!" He searched the Diplomat's coat pockets and found the envelope, a pen and a single key. He took the Diplomat's watch, and stepped back.

"Coat. Shirt. Tie. Undershirt," the boy said, pointing the gun.

The Diplomat removed each article.

"Shoes," the boy commanded. "Socks."

The Diplomat slipped off his shoes and bent over and removed his socks.

"Would you leave me without dignity?" he asked.

"Head down," the boy said. "Pants too."

The boy waved the gun.

The Diplomat heard snickering from the hallway behind him.

"Go!" the boy shouted, but the Diplomat didn't move.

His large pale body dwarfed the boy.

His pants lay crumpled at his feet.

"Leave!" the boy shouted again, pointing the gun at the Diplomat's face.

The Diplomat's voice quavered. "My place is here, with you."

The boy kicked the Diplomat's pants aside and came closer, raising the gun to the side of the Diplomat's face. When he fired beyond him, a gigantic clap sounded and the Diplomat recoiled. His head rang, a blaring hollow in his left ear followed by a piercing wail. He fell to the ground and scrambled on all fours, bruising his ankles and knees, the heels of his hands. He smelled gunpowder and clutched at his ear where blood filled the well. He made it to the corner of the nearest building. The boy raised the weapon and fired again. The Diplomat scrambled, rose, and ran shirtless and with no pants through the city. When he reached the vicinity of the embassy, he crouched behind a stone wall to gather his breath. On his knees he leaned his shoulder into the wall and pressed his hands to his lips.

THEY MOVED then in their opposite directions.

The boy traversed the city north with his companion.

The Diplomat went back to the embassy where he slowly dressed himself again. Clean white shirt and grey slacks. Blue suitcoat and red tie. He stood barefoot in his office and looked out to a thick line of smoke on the horizon. The pads of his feet were damaged. He lifted the receiver to his good ear. The line was dead. The tanks were gone. A plane flew overhead and a concussive force met the air, followed by a deafening explosion that shook the foundations of the building and shed dust from the ceiling beams. In the near distance a burgeoning of light and hoary smoke fired the sky, the brilliance hungry as it engulfed brush and buildings, house and fence and vine. Placing his hands wide on the window, he watched the tree before him flare to an immutable bloom. The light leapt up and set the peaked gables aglow. The glass became nearly unbearable, but the Diplomat held fast, witnessing a desolation magnificent and irrevocable.

On the wide plain beyond the city the white flamingos with black beaks turned their heads upward and lifted, nosing north in an undulant swirl that pushed at the night until the birds appeared as a single raft in the sky. A murmur of wings, dim and opalescent, filled the earth with longing, and over all a darkness as of the advent of creation hovered until at last the travelers made out the stars that wheeled overhead like a silver river harkening them on.

CITY ON THE THRESHOLD OF STARS

PANEL 1

I.

1942. Over the wide grey ocean back to Prague
and the River Vltava in central Bohemia,
the Mother of Cities, the Golden City,
City on the Threshold of Stars.
To Nazi occupation where I wonder
where I came from and watch the world grow
smaller and bigger at once, the violent

enthroned in the seat of nations, a tongue for the song
of women and men, to halt the old order
and inscribe the new with consuming fire.
  Jan Kubiš and Jozef Gabčík, soldiers, sons of Czech, born
for a day when the body rises and kills
and the mouth long silent shouts vengeance to the sky.
My three daughters were not yet born. My three daughters

were yet to be when an entire city was lost. Removed
from the face of the earth. My grandfather Herbert is
        German.
My grandmother Catherine is Czech. The cloth they wore
        was common.

In secret the Czech king commissioned Jan and Jozef
to travel nocturnal by foot and boat,
over mountains and rivers through the dark west
to England, to be welcomed
by the old-century Royal Air Force and given the new science
to return to their besieged country, hunt, find, and destroy
the devil Heydrich, the Nazi warlord, the Butcher of Prague.

II.

City on a hill, Lidice, small Prague on the flat south
of the high mountains called Pyratetten. Teeth of the Sky.
Of Czech blood venerable, laid bare, and borne of love.
By faith the Czechs believed. By fate it came to be.
Nazi onslaught obscuring day, bearing night
to the capital city of nations, Prague, foreign
tanks and airbirds, fears and terrors, skies filled

of fire and screaming bombs, wind-cleavers,
the cry of children and the mother's wail,
mobs, sirens, no water, thirst,
they covered their heads, suffered, waited
for England, for allies,
but in the end their land was taken.
The unthinkable, to be lost to Germany.

My young daughter once said: You're my favorite Daddy in
        the stars.
She didn't know how Prague and her people sought Heydrich,
        the Blond Beast,
to take his life, and return him whole to hell—the familiar
        hand

of the final solution, the uniform he kept clean,
narrow-nosed man whose wife, dog-eyed and supple,

reminded the living of another Nazi frau

who made lampshades of Jewish skin, Hangman Heydrich

who adored power, wanted his boss Himmler's life,

and took the ancient throne of the Bohemian kings

at Hradschin Castle high over the St. Charles Bridge.

III.

My daughters didn't know to emulate the Fuhrer.
Heydrich slaughtered Czechs. Jan, of average height,
thin-faced, serious, Jozef, bigger, boisterous,
wide-chested, willing when called to forfeit their lives.
Tomorrow we end it, Jan shouted
over the propeller noise.
Tomorrow, Jozef answered.

He looked to the eyes of his friend.
Are you afraid?
Jan took Jozef's face in his hands.
Today we die well my friend.
Their clothing was dark,
the face of Heydrich emblazoned
in the mind's eye as the aircraft droned on.

Why do I love you so? I asked my daughter, three times.
"Because God made you to love me," she said, and still so
        young
she didn't yet know how fully, how completely, beautiful
        things synchronize.

When the Nazis invaded the Czech lands

my Czech grandmother married my German grandfather
in New York City where they danced
and heard little word of their home countries
but let their bodies flare like flame
in the dark of the dance hall
as they tipped their heads to the light
and kissed fiercely. I am German. I am Czech.

IV.

Night drop at low altitude in a British plane,
two men on strings fell down and down
in darkness, the land below like a lost love, *laskah*,
returned to the earth effortless
as shadows. Near invisible, near light
the men ran as those who know their enemy
and whose desire is to destroy him.

On a morning in May when Heydrich drove
his green Mercedes coupe
toward the Castle in Prague, the two leapt
from a corner, concealed, lofted
their British-made bomb and blew
the rear of the car to pieces, shattering Heydrich's spine.
The Butcher wrinkled his nose. Groans slipped from the slit
      of his mouth.

Fire, whispered Jan, and Jozef beheld the beauty
billowing, mixed with smoke, a red black column
tunneling the sky. Can we ever really know

each other? My daughters. Me. The men who fled
cursing Heydrich in his death
throes, leaving him for what they hoped
was God's reckoning, the uniform he kept clean,

blood-soaked, tattered, the Butcher's body, the Butcher's face.
He breathed for ten days and when he died of his wounds
Hitler summarily executed 1,331 Czechs.

V.

201 women among them. The Nazis besieged
Jan and Jozef and others of the Czech resistance
in the Karl Borromaeus Church, and no Czechs came out
alive. The Germans took 3000 Jews from the safe ghetto
at Theresienstadt and herded them East to be exterminated.
500 of the 600 at large Jews in Berlin were imprisoned
and on the day of Heydrich's death 152 were executed.

Can we ever forget the small village, Lidice,
near the mining town Kladno, and how the Germans marched
to avenge Heydrich? The town 12 miles from Prague.
The raiment, the clothing of the children—no one knows
where it went. To our shame now we have nearly forgotten
Hitler's orders: 1. Execute all men by shooting.

2. Send all women to concentration camps.

3. Concentrate the children. Those capable of
being Germanized send to SS families in
Germany.

4. Burn the town and level it to the ground.

Three days after Heydrich's heart stopped,
ten flights of German Security Police
under the command of Captain Max Rostock took
formation around the village.
Nine years later Rostock hung by the neck in Prague
but first from the bullhorn
his electric voice

PANEL 3

VI.

in the German tongue:

Alles muss hier bleiben. Everyone stays.

Keine gehen. No one goes. From dawn to dusk

Nazi soldiers led boy and man to the garden behind the
      Mayor's barn

to be shot by firing squad at close range. Tap, tap, tap.

Three bullets: head, chest, chest. Ten of the living at a time.

      172

men and boys. Their bodies like leaves on the ground.

      Spiritbone.

The German Police took seven Lidice women to Prague

and shot them in public. City of One-hundred Spires. The
      remainder,

195 women in all, they sent to Ravensbrueck

where seven met the gas chamber,

three disappeared,

and 42 expired from concentration camp conditions.

Of the Lidice women, an unlucky four were pregnant,

my daughters still don't know those women

were taken to a hospital in Prague, their children forcibly
      aborted,

the women shipped empty to Ravensbrueck.

I hope my daughters never know how the Germans took the
  living children
of Lidice, 90 in all.
I am Czech. Spiritbone. I am German.
From these, Himmler's "racial experts"
deemed eight children sound, garment of praise,
and they were sent to Germany to be raised German with
  German names.
Ingested into the Fatherland through the Nazi program
  Lebensborn.

VII.

The remaining 82 children were taken by train to Lodz
where they lived three weeks in a collection camp,
the youngest, only a year and six days old,
the oldest boys fourteen, the oldest girls fifteen.
In early June they arrived at a castle where they
were told to undress, keep only underwear, a towel,
and a bar of soap for a shower before the journey to Chelmno.

The children were then squeezed into the closed bed of a
        truck
modified to fit 90 bodies and killed by exhaust in eight
        minutes.
My three daughters are Czech. My three daughters are
        German.
Natalya. Ariana. Isabella. When you were born I kissed the
        skin
on the inside of your wrists and whispered, I will love you
        forever.
How like your mother you are! So ready to defend mankind.
I see you hand in hand looking out over the edge

of the world to a land beyond our reach. At war's end
no trace of Lidice remained: the houses bonfired, the ruins
        dynamited, the rubble covered by landfill. All men
        killed. All women and children abducted, forsaken,

or exterminated.

The earth under storm and rain, snow and broken tree, a rose
	garden,
silence. The ground the garment of praise instead of the spirit
	of despair.
As late as 1947 the last women of Lidice sent newspaper pleas
through Allied media into post-war German homes:
*My city was lost. My child taken. Please return my child. I
	am from Lidice.*
*Our husbands were shot. Our children lost. Have mercy on
	us.*
And some few boy-children were returned home not knowing
	their mothers' names.

VAPOR

What is your life? You are just a vapor that appears for a little while and then vanishes.

—James 4:14

Love is, that you are the knife which I plunge into myself.

—Franz Kafka

LOVE IS BLINDNESS

I

IN THE BEGINNING Michael White and Kristina Rosamonde loved each other.

He'd fallen for her because she was high-boned and thin, a reminder of a beauty he'd never possessed but longed for all his life. And certainly, when they began he felt he was more than a man in her presence, still awkward and strong, but with a near feline resonance then that seemed to radiate from her to him. Road builder, do-it-all construction worker and cabinet maker from out near Pray, Montana, past the long bend of the Yellowstone where the land went to wilderness and water moved like an ancient secret into mountains and carved rock. Since he met her he saw beauty all around him. Before her he'd loved women, but they had not loved him. With women and work he'd always walked with his head bowed, his massive shoulders bent inward as if to protect and shield his heart.

But loving her made him almost fearless. Love, the most primal emotion.

AT THE START her love was everything to him, she thought.

Now it wrecked him.

She admitted she'd loved him truly, even as she curled herself into a tidy ball in the leather chair and watched the darkened hearth. The heat of old fires had become mounds of ash below the log grate, like the infinitesimal mountains of a people too small to be seen. She rose and crossed the room. The sun reddened toward evening. The earth was dark in the east. She approached the dance floor he'd built for her, a floor of immaculate lacquered pine, a twenty by twenty-foot floated space, mirrored foot to ceiling on one wall, the slender arm of the barre horizontal in the expanse. She stretched her arms overhead one at a time and then ran them the length of her legs until she put her palms on the floor. Normally she felt lovely when she stretched, beholden to a power she expressed easily, never doubting the natural upswell of the body and the loading it went through before the dance began, her movements like a sprung rhythm, a rhythm ready to be sprung, back-stretched and back bent in beveled bell-like curves that seemed to attend her the way light attended morning.

But today, and seemingly for days on end now, her body fought her. She felt unbendable. She knew she'd altered interiorly. She'd become rigid, less agile. Less forgiving.

She stood before the window, watching the horizon, remembering. For her part, she'd loved him more than she thought possible, with a cherished sense of abandon. Dance instructor for Ballet Arts in Bozeman, she was capable of fine sissonnes and soaring grand jetés for which she'd been called "physical," "entrancing," and "leonine" on the stages of New York, Denmark and Russia. She'd felt fully adored in his presence. They lived together in Pray, an hour's drive from Bozeman on a dirt road through the Bridger Mountains.

He had one good eye, and one damaged in childhood by an errant tree limb, and if he'd been anything he'd been completely given to love her, as if his one good eye saw more than most people saw with two. He smelled of wood and forest, dry fern and timothy grass. She'd fallen for his big frame, a pure convergence with hers, and she had loved him for his humility, his grace. In fact, she'd always felt she would accomplish love, a bold true marital love. She felt as strongly independent as the next person, but she wasn't afraid to believe in marriage. She'd do it differently than her parents, she thought. Better. She never wanted to be one of the multitudes who went down, consumed by the excruciating fracture of a failed union.

She shook out her arms and legs and tried to loosen whatever gripped her.

Unsatisfied, she sat down in the chair again and tried to breathe.

The music was a Bach piece she'd chosen even after their fight last night—a composition called *Jesu, Joy of Man's Desiring*, the 10th movement of a cantata whose alternate structure was like the architecture of flight, while their fighting was a descent increasingly more vengeful that kept leading them, against her will, down into an abyss from which they might never return. She believed she still loved him, but with his obstinacy and his growing desire to subdue her, she was losing sight of their future. He knew her eccentricities and character flaws, and even her wholly unforeseen moment of abject weakness six months ago when she had forsaken him for someone else, and this, she thought, would be their demise. He had wanted complete honesty. So had she. Before they met she'd had her lovers, and he, amazingly, had been a virgin. The compact they made was absolute. They'd agreed like two souls who wanted only that which is eternal. And now he couldn't overcome what she'd told him.

Her father, a former dancer himself, had been serially unfaithful to her mother, and still she heard his clipped accent, "The alignment of muscle and artistry has no song but its own." It reminded her of the rich tonality of Michael's voice when he had approached her back in the early days after he'd seen her dance with the Montreal Ballet in Chicago. "You are a miracle," he'd said, and she noticed in his eyes a loneliness in which she felt so loved she thought her heart would split in two. His gaze then held something delicate and true, and it hurt to remember it, like a stab wound, she thought, but calcified, a harder, darker shard of ice into the ice she already knew.

Back then she'd turned from him, wiping her eyes, and gone backstage to gather herself. They'd only known each other three months but the ultimate progression rushed over them, they fell in love, their polar physicality hemming them to one another as if in a single garment, their way with one another a totality, she thought, like the ornate baroque tapestries of the National Museum in Copenhagen. She was barely over five feet tall and thin as a willow. He was six foot four and two-hundred forty pounds. She envisioned her small body alongside his, her light hand over the density and darkness of his workman's skin. He was white but ruddy, almost slate-colored with the acts he performed in dirt and oil and tar, road construction, house building, interiors, landscaping, roof work. She loved trying to reconcile their binary fortitude: her mind of high art; his will to bend earth. Her music and many-toned elegance. His water, wood, and stone.

They'd met in a shoe repair shop in Bozeman off Main Street, the Spanish Peaks framed through the window behind his head.

"Where are you from?" he'd asked. "You're a dancer. I see it in your walk, in how you move your hands."

She loved his plainspoken directness.

"I am," she said. "And you?"

She knew he couldn't be, as big as he was.

"No," he answered, smiling.

"I can teach you," she said, mimicking his matter-of-fact tone.

"No you can't," he said, and they both laughed.

She knew now she hadn't taught him to dance, except with their mutual shadow.

She'd shown him the silk ribbons of her point shoes back then. Beheld his large, rugged boots as if made of bear hide and barbed wire. She'd come to Montana from Los Angeles to escape her family, perhaps herself. His family, immigrants three generations removed, was Czech and German, linear, staid, but he'd taken to her with an openness she'd nearly lusted for, and it wasn't a year before he married her. The wedding took place in a basin of cottonwoods along the Yellowstone west of Carter's Bridge outside Livingston. Her veil captured the wind and she'd never before felt more opaque or more beautiful. He lifted her in his arms, whooped for joy, carried her to his old Chevy truck, and placed her on the bench seat beside him. From there they drove to the house he'd hewn of log and rock north of Pray where they made their start at a life together.

NOW THEY'D been together seven years.

She hated how ill thoughts could be stacked one upon another like poorly laid brick until they collapsed, killing the beloved in the rubble. She didn't sleep well, and doubted he did either, her mind plagued by accusation and affront, his body more granite than man. In fact, she couldn't recall the last good night's sleep she had. Early this morning when he strode out the door mumbling something about "wood" and "fire," she'd watched him duck through the frame resolute as a soldier. She wanted to stop him, curse him. Since the revelation, he couldn't stop belittling her, and normally she just retreated and sat in the leather chair, her limbs wrapped to her chest, her arms tightly laced around her legs.

Long ago, when she first kissed him, his kiss was like the water of apples.

Now her heart smoked in her chest.

3

SHE WAS convinced they were colluding, wickedly, to sabotage themselves.

The thought made her stand and move with a brisk gait back to the dance floor. She held her chin high and her lips full so that in profile she was the image of a marble sculpture or a painting of a woman imbued with a power she concealed, from a source she alone knew. She paused, staring at her face in the mirror. Had she *ever* hated this much? Had she ever been so hated? His punishing edicts boiled inside her. His misogynous self-pity and stonewalling, naming her weak and heartless, calling her *abusive*, even *whorish*. Water came to her eyes.

She turned and looked out the window, to the river and the mountain beyond. He was out there. She'd gone with him often and waited until he was done, helping him load the truck with split wood. When he threw the blade, the wood shouted. The image of him chopping down trees was emblazoned in her mind's eye. Today he was alone. No, she reasoned, she had never felt such annihilating hatred. Even before she confessed the affair, he had nearly forced her to leave, his defensiveness laced with what she felt to be insurmountable rage; her own burgeoning contempt and criticism like hooks that leapt from her tongue and took to his skin like hornets. But after her mea culpa, the war made an ascension she regretted. Bitterness had erected a home in her as ancient as the cliff fortress of Edinburgh. Slight upon slight, hatred begetting hatred.

The nature of light was prismatic. The absence of light, darkness.

She needed to dance. His whiteness had obliterated her. His closed system sensibilities, insatiable in black and white. But admittedly, her color had shattered him too. Her flight like a crane through mist, her mystery.

Swiftly she angled to the floor and leapt upward in a pirouette, powerful and smooth as water. "Reminiscent of Baryshnikov," the curator of the Bolshoi Theater in Moscow had whispered to her when she was young. She landed and spun like a vertical arrow until she flared low again, horizontal to the floor as she placed a fist to the hardwood, her right leg flush beneath her, her left suspended parallel to the arm she held in second position. I will break my body to my own will, she thought.

She wasn't young anymore. The coil in her tightened. In response she danced harder, with greater tenacity, and when the steel of her body resisted her she contemplated throwing herself into the mirror. Instead she ran the length of the floor and leapt on a diagonal into the air before falling to the floor, weeping.

After the affair, she tried to touch him, tried to move his enmity to mercy. In fact, she'd glided over his still form with an overt and ethereal wildness.

"I'm here for you!" she said, she'd whispered it, then proclaimed it loudly.

But he would not be moved.

Now she despised herself for it. In her heart of hearts, she also despised her own father, even after witnessing her mother draw near to him in the end. After all his infidelities her mother didn't flee, but rather came close, clinging to him in the long march of the disease that took his life. He'd come to Los Angeles through Spain by way of Mexico. An orphan of Mexican descent, adopted by Catalan high bloods, he'd studied at Barcelona's illustrious Studio de la Esperanza, ending his career as the artistic director for the San Francisco Ballet before retiring to Los Angeles. Out the broad vertical windows that abutted the edge of the dance floor her view took in the width of the water as it bent away from the house. The river was blood red and aglow. The sun's light flooded the room. Giant rock shelves overhung the river, and beyond them where the mountain stood inviolable she saw a wonder of beauty immediate and immense. Her mother's transparency shamed her. Like knife and sharpening stone, the way her mother lived without a bone of vengeance in her body cut Kristina now. She imagined Michael and the nautilus his arms made of the axe. She imagined him carving a path through the forest, a swath of grief to a point of no return.

4

HE WAS FAR from home, the sun falling in the southwest quadrant of the sky. He thought his blade could be likened to a kind of truth that tore men asunder. He held the axe in his hand and eyed the long handle, an elegant but fortified limb of wood worn at the grip, smooth in the palm. Seven years. Could she be who she said she was? Loyal, after what she'd done? In a mighty thrust sideways he swung the axe in both hands and felt the blade bite the wood.

He never imagined his heart could hurt him so much. He'd taken love, and marriage, for granted. He thought it would be easier; he wasn't dumb, he knew it took work; but this was beyond his worst fears, and now he thought he might wilt under it if he didn't get more physical. All he'd ever wanted was to please her. He didn't care about other people's perceptions. But about loyalty he cared more than a ravenous wolf cared about hunger.

With his good eye he managed to take in the small vista of his world, the tree, the blade, the fresh split of wood that oozed and gave off scent now high and sweet and beaded with sap. In grade school the nurse had told him his left eye was useless. He loosened the tree's hold and pulled the blade free and gathered and cut into the bole again until the wedge began to form and the bright chips fanned around him like a wing at his feet. The work felt good to him, the body a well-oiled instrument until at last the great tree creaked and leaned and the long slow descent was followed by a loud, Whump! A sense of wind. The ground rumbled beneath him. He'd felled a large black pine. Kristina was lost to him.

Before sundown he'd have the tree sectioned and split.

He'd get the truth from her, he thought, and when she gave him the truth he'd claim vengeance; he'd do finally the horrible thing he neither desired nor feared. He thought of her strengthless father. Wronging her mother whenever he damn well pleased. Michael told himself he was not afraid to tear life from the chest of the man Kristina had lain with and watch his small spirit flee through a rift in the curtain of the world.

No, he countered, he didn't want that, and hoped he would not be able to perform the deed his jealousy conceived. He just wanted her back. But she was so distant now, and in his sorrow he had come to believe it was himself and no other who had placed her there. His insatiable cruelty.

Even now her hands still searched him. His body, his face.

But he'd warned her, hadn't he? Yet it came, the terrible happenstance in which she'd placed him between the rock of his love for her and the hard place of his friendship with Damon. The one he wanted dead now. At first he'd foregone revenge and had not in fact mentioned it to Damon, only eyed him with violence and seen the mortal fear in Damon's eyes and let it rest. But after six months now, Michael was still unable to surmount the thoughts that covered his mind like locusts. Her lips tasting of wine. Thoughts of her naked in a cry of pleasure, almost agony, not with him but with Damon.

Closer than a brother.

He'd known Damon since boyhood.

They'd worked fields and dug ditches. They'd roofed and built houses and grated roads. They were hired everywhere they went and kept pace with each other, and every boss they'd ever known wanted to keep them on. But it ended on the flat surface of the industrial plaza off the frontage road six months back, a week after she'd confessed. Tar to their elbows, Michael had looked up to where Damon blocked the sun and forced himself to listen as Damon wept and spoke like a child.

"I don't know what to say," Damon said. His face cut by shadow.

"Speak your mind, Damon," Michael said.

Damon wrung his hands.

"Say what you need to."

"Your wife," Damon said. "Me."

"Stop," Michael said. "Don't talk anymore." Like walking through the center of a forge, he felt white-hot. He radiated fire. Striding to the edge of the roof, he descended the ladder, and vowed never to speak to Damon again.

When he had arrived home, Kristina was in the kitchen.

From the hall he called to her. "Damon told me today."

She turned and approached him with tears in her eyes.

His own face broke and he couldn't bear it so he walked back out of the house and drove three days into Canada.

When he returned he promised himself he'd put it behind him.

But he did no such thing.

A physical wrath would be needed, he thought, to undo what had already been done.

In the months since, he'd been controlling her to her whit's end. Threatening her with his voice at such a volume her responses came to him even here in the forest as he threw steel to wood. "You make me crazy. Don't shut me down. Don't push me away. It happened once. I was drunk."

She's married to me, and no one else, he reminded himself.

He pictured her in swan's array with the New York City Ballet at the Lincoln Center when she'd been called for a run of Tchaikovsky's masterpiece. He'd been in the front row in a tuxedo, the bone-colored Stetson at rest on his knees, his feet decked out in dark boots and he'd forgotten everything in the whole world but the form of her and her precision and the revelation of her emotion in the end of Tchaikovsky's final ascent. During the ovation he'd stood with tears streaming down his face and watched her collarbones rise and fall and heard the massive swell of the crowd, a crescendo that took a long time dying. It was her soul he loved, as intimate and unconquerable as any wilderness.

I'm no angel, he reckoned.

But never, *never* was I unfaithful.

He'd make her tell him the whole truth tonight. She'd tell the truth, and he'd do what his body was meant to do. Men wanted her cream-brown skin and blood red lips, her eyes light blue and severe as the sapphires in Montana's mountains. They wanted to steal her away and secure her in the crown of their affections. God had not given him a giant's body for nothing. He'd do a giant's work.

Still, he thought, he shouldn't kill.

He wanted to return to her, to where he needed to be. But grace eluded him.

"I can't take it," she said three months ago. "I need to forgive myself."

"Forgive *yourself*?" he'd shouted. "What about me? You should beg *my* forgiveness."

On the slant of the mountain he swung the axe. He felt like a whipped child. The memory of what she'd spoken next desolated him. "I do beg your forgiveness," she'd said and taken his face in her hands. "Forgive me. Please forgive me. I beg you." Her sincerity had caused a great well of shame in him. At first, he thought he would receive her, but instead he'd run from the house again. And when he regained himself, he'd dug in opposite her until now, until tonight when she would need to admit what he felt sure was the truth. That she'd forsaken him not just once with Damon but many times, and with others too. He thought of his own father's violence. The supposed tree that took his eye. No one escapes their own father, he thought. No one.

Tonight, she would speak true.

He trembled. He raised the axe and let it fall. In the smoke of late summer fires his tongue tasted ash. If she denies again, she stays and I go, he told himself. I will go to where I can't be found. He let the blade rest and pulled his shirt over his head and threw the shirt on a nearby crown of brush. He stood with the heel of his hand on the axe butt and eyed the land and felt its evening glow, a raiment over his shoulders. Behind him the mountain was a massive bulwark, the water below silver and flushed red, bleeding to black. He'd misjudged the angle of the sun. The sky would go dark before he finished, before he was able to load the truck and turn toward home.

He couldn't abide sharing her. "You're mine," he'd told her early in the marriage.

She had stared at him then, saying, "*No es verdad.* I am no man's possession."

He wanted to agree with her but the seed of doubt had grown into a wicked tree that set down its limbs around them and pierced their skin. He felt weary. Early, the thought of her dancing on the floor he'd crafted for her made him feel good down to his bones. She used to touch her face to his every day, her scent the scent of lilac and cherry blossoms. She hadn't danced in the house for what seemed to him a long while.

He ground the grit from his throat, tilted the axe overhead and split wood with a force that made the cleavings fly ten feet from the chopping block.

Finally he set the axe shallow into the wood, on a slant sideways to the earth. He sat on the ground and put his head down. He decided he could not do what he intended.

5

WHEN HE entered the house, the lights were off.

He didn't see her.

"Kristina," he called.

"Here," she answered. She was seated in the chair, her body a fortress.

The entirety of their existence pivoted around a single act.

He wanted to be kind to her.

Instead he approached her directly and accused her not only of infidelity with Damon, but of wanton, willful lechery. When his voice flared, she watched his neck thicken. But when he barked the words "bitch" and "slut," she rose, stepped up onto the arm of the chair and flung her arm wide, raking the side of his face over his good eye, a strike so firm her nails felt like a disc tilling a field.

She grabbed at his torso as she landed, but already he was on his knees, clutching his head and crying out. When he was finally able to open his eye the entire thing was red with blood.

Seeing nothing, he looked out at her, weeping.

His groans were guttural sounds that made her weep as well.

"I can't see," he said, shaking. "We need to go now."

"Yes," she answered.

It took a long time for him to rise, and when he was upright she walked him down the hall and to the front door. He moved slowly, his head bent forward in his hands. She placed a rag over his eye and told him to keep it compressed.

At the truck, she pushed on his shoulders to get him into the passenger seat. He seemed to resist but she succeeded in positioning him enough to close the door.

She sped the highway east to Livingston.

He was quiet as he entered the assigned room.

Quiet as he waited, and as he heard the doctor enter.

"What do we have?" the doctor said, setting the rag aside, opening the eye with a gloved hand.

"Feels like splinters of wood," Michael said, "Across the surface and bunched up under the eyelid." The doctor looked in with a bright light. Shook his head. He hunched his shoulders, shook his head again.

"Come with me," he told Michael.

He fixed his eyes on Kristina and said, "I'll bring him back in a moment."

The doctor led Michael to another room and closed the door.

"How did this happen?"

"Accident," said Michael.

"What kind of accident?" the doctor asked.

"Tree branch," Michael answered.

The doctor went quiet. "Appears to have been more human than that," he said.

"It wasn't," said Michael and they stood in silence until the doctor led him back to Kristina, where the doctor peered closely at her face before he turned to Michael again. He placed gauze over the eye and wrapped the skull crosswise. "Let it heal some, and report back to me in a few days."

As Michael stood before her in the parking lot he was like a boy, she thought. He held his body like a man, but his head made him look boyish. She believed she'd crushed him then, performed in him a ruin she did not imagine possible. Yet on the ride home she also thought she recognized softness, his chin a little more forward, his head a little more erect as the ride progressed.

But when he lay in their bed that night his resignation unraveled her. She sat beside him and didn't touch him. When she spoke he gave no response. His anger seemed remote now, like heat at the core of the earth.

Three days later when the patch came off and the doctor ran Michael through the visual test, she was devastated.

"Zero percent," the doctor said. "No visual capacity."

6

FOR DAYS her mind played tricks. As she watched Michael move fatally through the house she told herself she deserved his worst. She told herself he'd disliked her for years, and reckoned his blindness with his rage, blaming herself for both. But he wasn't without fault, she reasoned. Hadn't he bit her with a venom that poisoned who they were? He'd been very cruel, even before her faithlessness.

She'd been losing her love for him for longer than she wanted to admit.

In bed when she drew near and saw his shoulder blades illumined by moonlight, she wondered at her incapacity to feel. There should be more to us, she thought, I should be more, and when she thought this way she wanted to come near to him again and open his arms and sink into his chest.

An axe to break the frozen seas of the soul. Where had she heard those words? She couldn't recall, but they arrived like velvet in her hands. That axe would be made of light, she thought, and governed by light's properties. Early on, he had broken all the ice in her. He'd overcome everything, lifting her to plateaus of affection she had not thought possible after the harshness of her family, her classical training, the foreclosed and fortified patterns of her parents and how her own internal circumambulations echoed the loneliness of her successes through America and Europe, Munich, Amsterdam, Prague, Moscow. Nothing satisfied. Except the care she and Michael had shown each other. His hands had lifted her, and he'd drawn himself into her with such hope and gentleness she'd felt aware of a presence between them not unlike what she'd known at night as a child in the mountains above Barcelona under the great tilt of stars.

She attributed it to his upbringing the deep-toned and archaic lines he'd spoken over her which never failed to spring her wide open. *"Fear not, for you will not be ashamed. With great compassion I will gather you. My love will not depart from you."* He didn't have the language of harshness then, only generosity. He listened and loved, and his joy accompanied them often, as if flowing from an inexhaustible wellspring. He had been something more to her, warming and delighting her and destroying all she'd known of loss, creating from the wreckage something infinite.

She knew he had felt the same about her.

Now she watched him as he walked sightlessly across the dance floor and set himself down at the edge of it and let the morning sun warm his face. She remembered how her mother's loving kindness had stepped forth when the final exhalation began. Her mother and father had met in Madrid, married in Barcelona, retired finally to the City of Angels. Her mother a lofty white Angelino, daughter of the architect who designed the L.A. Museum of Art and Urban Light. Kristina's father elected for hospice, and not only did her mother agree, she had the small spinet piano moved into the bedroom where she played Brahms and Strauss for him, the point and counterpoint of Bach and the quiet orchestral sweep of Dvorak's *Rusalka*. He'd slept intermittently through the days. At night she lay with him and he held her, and he was tender in the holding. She'd seen her mother kiss her father's mouth, caress his face. And when Kristina found them this way she felt not only heartbreak but something akin to peace.

Setting her eyes on Michael in the sunlight now, she found him beautiful.

His face was calm. He appeared to smile upon her. The heart of the man she thought harbored only hate for her, worked in her now and in fact the stillness of his presence led to her courage, for when she approached and looked closely at his face she desired only to bring him to her and draw the pain up out of him.

The body surrenders, she thought.

And surrender is what we need. Now. As if to carry us from death to life. She had experienced such surrender at the Mariinsky Theatre of the Imperial Ballet in St. Petersburg, the building a four-tiered marvel with flying buttresses in the dome and a high ceiling from which hung a majestic fifty-foot chandelier. The U-shaped archways of the balconies were also bedecked with chandeliers. The stage lit, the auditorium black, the music had brought her into a depth of darkness to which she'd given herself so fully that when she emerged into the eternal embrace of the Prince in the final repetition of the leitmotif from the *Lake of the Swans* she stared into the void with tears streaming down her face. Her arms in a raised oval over the arabesque, head tipped back to the curve of his shoulder, their chests heaving with exhaustion, the crowd roared and she was lost and alone and the sound swept her into an intimacy of witness in which she thought she might forsake the world and everything in it.

Such a moment, she thought, came once in a lifetime.

Yet as she watched Michael now, the moment was present to her again.

She went to him and knelt beside him and took his face in her hands.

7

HE DID NOT move away.

Her genuine caress made him cry, and he bent over then and convulsed as she held his face and kissed his cheek. They grew still, listening. Finally, when he laid down on his side she placed his head in her lap and he wept silently as she pressed her cheek to his cheek. At last she closed his eyes with her fingers and kissed his eyelids, whispering the words she'd heard her own mother speak to her father before dying, light words of an indelible tongue.

"Let me kiss you with the kisses of my mouth."

Kristina kissed Michael's lips, and again, his eyelids.

"Your love is more delightful than wine."

—for John Stands In Timber

SPIRIT OF THE ANIMAL

The Cheyenne have a tradition of a golden age when war was unknown and universal peace prevailed. All strangers met in friendship and parted on good terms. Such a far off time when hostile encounters were unknown, is told of by many of the tribes of the northern plains.

—George Bird Grinnell

I

FAR FROM camp, a light snow fell and he tied his horse to track on foot. Night. The land robed in white. On the border of a vast forest, close upon two deer, he crossed a path of paw-prints, clawed and slightly weighted down. Prints fresh and firmly indented on the snow's surface. He paused. Good-sized, he thought. He knew the animal. Silver, he thought, and black. Like quick death beneath a heavy robe.

He knelt to the earth and touched at the tracks and thought of his father, a kind of effigy of all this wilderness, man of cities, son of the son of an émigré from Czech-Austrian empires, of the surname Chandler, candle maker, European, white, distant, unaware, the father with whom he hadn't spoken for fifteen years, the father who he himself had fought in the mud of St. Louis. After the fight, and the blood-wound, Jeroen had left his father and long-dead mother and come west, the land bearing him whole to these mountains where he'd effectively rid himself of all who knew him. Forsaking them, he called himself brother to no one. Brother to vengeance. Brother of oblivion.

Kneeling, he let his index finger trace the outline of the paw print near his foot but before he rose the animal came from the forest, slashing his face and head, quick lines above the right ear, skin torn to the bone. Cold night, bright bone, hot blood from the skull, down his neck. I am made of paper, he thought. He turned and faced the animal, opened his fists and bared his teeth. He hands were hateful. His mouth made hard violent sounds.

Along a thin coulee to the south, Bird In Ground heard the white man and looked up from her horse. His body stood outlined against forest, steam from his wounds, pale breath above him. Hair a black mane, thick-barbed and crow-like to the mid-back. It was not her manner to be given in this way, but now that she he had found him, she said to herself, here we begin. Out two days scouting buffalo, she'd seen his horse's hoof prints and decided to trail the white man. Just before dusk she'd watched him running low and fast on a mantle of snow at Little Creek, tracing the line of the forest, tracking. Night now and in the dark she witnessed his movements and he was like the wolf to her and she felt strength in her heart, and it had been long since she felt such strength, and she was pleased. She saw Wolverine in the land also, claws like arrows in the man's flesh, the animal's mouth colored of the man's blood. The white man circled and danced, parried, attacked. Along the line of a draw, she sat still atop her horse, watching until the man's body was spent and Wolverine lay still, and the man fell to the ground next to the animal, and both lay still.

Approaching, she dismounted. He had used no weapon. She knelt and listened for his breath. She touched his face. His eyes were closed, the body still. He goes to the house of dawn, she thought. She drew herself over him and placed her head on his chest.

Quiet, the chamber of the spirit, quiet the blood of man. She stood again. Taking an eagle fan from the pouch at her side, she waved it above him, praying. She laid herself over him again, matching form to form, breathing quietly on his face. Slight weight on the chest, the closeness of her body, he drifted broken but not fully undone, eyes empty and blank and blind. With effort he opened them and stared. Her face was stark-boned and troubled, her look bent as if to say, Your life is not your own.

He closed his eyes and fell inward and down into a sleep that came like a pall draping the body whole, swift the black-winged bird, fearless the war animal that roams and purveys the soul, the body wracked and broken, broken off, ruined, razed, near dead but still alive and hungry in quick descent to the bottom. There as if up from beneath, vivid, numinous, his body seemed to speak the word surrender. Return. He exhaled with force and came breathing back into her hands.

SHE PRESSED her horse down near to him and drew the man over the shoulders of the horse and placed the body of Wolverine over the man's back. His horse followed hers. Night and day she rode and when she entered the fire of camp her people gathered and placed the two, man and Wolverine, inside the circle. She dismounted. Lifting her hands, she told how the white man wrestled Wolverine from the arc of the moon to the gray-black of dawn, killing Wolverine, then lying down to die. She let her hands fall. She motioned how he was brought back from death, and when she finished speaking to the people, she walked forward and whispered of him in the ear of her father.

THERE WAS NO good place to keep the white man, few or none trusting one of bright skin now after Sand Creek and the death that came there for Cheyenne women and children, the young men, the old. But Bird In Ground convinced her father they should keep him, and she was allowed to keep him.

For many turns of sun and moon the white man lay still in her father's lodge. Winter covered all in ice. Snow flew from skies of cloud and fog, burnished by sun, the canopy closed under an expanse of radiance, the snow a down-falling solemnity, vision near sightless, the blizzard white-blind and hushed, obscuring woman and man, children, land, stone and forest fallen to an end of falling until finally the sky broke wide as if torn and behind the veil, the world appeared crowned in bitter blue.

High in high winter, Jeroen was held in the mountain camp of the Cheyenne where he lay in the dark of Highwalker's lodge and Bird in Ground took the coat of Wolverine, setting it to stretch and dry. She lined the fringe with beadwork, the white tales of the martin, the blue-jay's bright-feathered fan. Her father saw and marveled and when the skin was ready she set it on the man's chest and he wore it heavy-laden, sunken-eyed until the spirit of the animal was soothed, and again a yearning was felt in the earth and sky, followed by the open-throated birds of day. Silver night, warm wind. The green of the world, and laughter, dance, song. In the early color, when the ground shone, and light grew more full, the white man gained his power again and in his dreams he rose up from his wounds, walking.

Highwalker went to see the white man's breath and stood before the white man and placed the back of his hand over the man's lips.

"Does he live?" he asked Bird In Ground.

The white man lay on a willow-rest bed.

"Yes," she said, placing her hand on the white man's chest.

As her father nodded, the white man opened his eyes and rose up and they murmured and she held the white man's hands. Inside the tipi he walked in a circle, returning heavy-headed to his bed. This occurred once, and again three days later, and from there each day he made his radius. More and more he seated himself around the fire. He watched Bird In Ground's hands over the clay cooking pots. He ate wild turnips, dried fruit, venison.

With his face turned to the ground, he chewed slowly.

Once when she touched the back of his head, he wept.

He had been alone on the earth.

He was no longer alone.

2

CHIEF HIGHWALKER. Of the four principle chiefs of the Cheyenne he was called great one, warrior, leader of the council of forty-four chiefs. Highwalker kept the strict form of governance of the Cheyenne nation, his wisdom was like the grey fox, his swiftness as the eagle, the bear.

Late summer, dry season of wind and fire Bird In Ground was given the white man to marry, and in a ceremony along the Powder River she lifted braids of sweetgrass, wafting smoke, white smoke offered in the four directions, upward into her breathing, into his. In Cheyenne she pronounced the words like wind and water, smooth stones bright in the river's bed. She looked and beheld the barren expanse of the plains. She had loved him first and brought him back from silence. She gave him his name now, a good name—*Vih-ho-wih Inshihwo-hihohts*—White Man Running.

LONG BEFORE in seasons of mourning and war, Bird In Ground, having lost a husband and two sons in the Sand Creek massacre, kept a war horse. Like Mochi. Like Chief Black Kettle's wife Woman Hereafter. And from that day she had gone with the others to kill white soldiers. One on the ridge at Two Medicine, two near the west fork of the Elktooth, arrows sent to the chest before they saw her, and when she reached them, her tomahawk swift at the base of the skull. There would be others, she thought.

But he was not like them. Not so white, he smelled of earth, and on their first night alone in the lodge she said, "I will be done with war." She gave her war horse to her father and joined herself to White Man Running. Among her people, she was revered, and Jeroen, having returned from his long sleep, felt awakened to new life. Like the sun, he walked from his own shadow.

He did not imagine love would come, and now he desired it more than all that came before. He gave himself wholeheartedly to her.

In the lodge before the fire he wondered at his life, white man born of a father long lost to him, son of cities, son even of the great city Prague, he remembered it from his father Aristos' and uncle Gabriel's old stories, tales spoken in a strange tongue, city on the threshold of stars, place of his great grandfather's birth and childhood in the old country, before passing over great waters to New York, choosing the name candle maker, Chandler, in order to hide the dynastic line and go alone to St. Louis on the edge of the wild vastness, there to bring forth sons Aristos and Gabriel, and there Aristos, American, married, and his wife gave birth to Jeroen, the new, on the edge of the unknown. Jeroen, after fighting his own father, lost himself in the wild where now he was found, in another place, with another people. He wanted what they gave. He wanted to live in the presence of Bird In Ground, with her father, her people.

Before he had seemed more animal than man. Now he wanted only life with her.

But his heart was haunted.

"NIGHTBORNE," the old women began to speak aloud when they saw him in camp. They turned their noses, calling him, "Closed-eye."

"Quiet," said the old men, "the animal leads him."

NIGHT'S darkness, only a short season from the day of their marriage, Bird In Ground let herself come up from sleep, though she knew she'd find him gone. She knew he traveled the earth without her, without anyone. She wondered at his path, and where it might lead.

She lay back with her face to the sky and sang her bear songs and the elk song.

3

LATE DARK, outside the main village Jeroen came to the war camp of Tall Bull, chief of the Dog Soldiers. Here the warriors were gathered, seated in a circle.

"*Hahmstoo-ists!*" said Tall Bull, motioning with his nose to White Man Running. "Sit with me. I will tell you a story." Tall Bull smoothed the ground in front of him with his hand. He made two marks in it with his right thumb, two with his left, and a double mark with both thumbs together. He rubbed his hands and passed his right hand up his right leg to his waist and touched his left hand and passed it up his right arm to his chest. He did the same on the other side. Then he touched the marks on the ground with both hands and passed his hands over his head before moving his hands over his entire body.

"The Creator is witness," Tall Bull said.

He looked at White Man Running and at the others. "When I was young I rode with Wolf Mule, White Antelope, and three Sioux warriors—Good Bear, Spotted Tail, and Yellow Eyes. We were scouts, young warriors, wolves sent to find the enemy camp, a war camp of the Pawnee." Tall Bull crouched, then stood, and pushing his right hand outward he said, "We moved swift as the hawk. But we found no camp." He walked in a circle. "Finally, we found a lone Pawnee on foot, carrying a bundle on his back, and from a sloped hill we charged. Seeing us, the Pawnee turned. He dropped his bundle and robe and ran directly toward us. Good Bear rode ahead to strike him, to count first coup, but the Pawnee shot Good Bear's horse dead with an arrow."

Jeroen watched Tall Bull, his body and hands, his hair.

"The horse drifted and fell, throwing Good Bear to the ground. White Antelope charged the Pawnee and the Pawnee shot his horse in the chest, making the horse fall away in a long arc. Finally, Wolf Mule rushed in and the Pawnee ran at him too. Wolf Mule's horse halted, turned around, and ran away. The Pawnee followed the horse, running upright and fast, drew his bow, and shot Wolf Mule. The arrow hit one of Wolf Mule's silver hair plates in the center, piercing it so the arrow entered his flesh, and stuck out from the middle of his back."

Tall Bull put his head down, shaking his hair so it covered his face. He bent his back. Slowly rocking back and forth, he said, "We gathered on horseback a little away, Good Bear behind Spotted Tail, Wolf Mule hunched over the mane of his horse, the arrow jutting up from his spine. We watched. We did not attack the Pawnee." Then Tall Bull stood straight, tall. "The Pawnee signed to us, saying: 'Come! Kill me! I am a chief. It will be a good thing for you if you kill me. If you do this, you have killed a chief.' The Pawnee yelled at us, pointing to the sky, 'I am like the sun! I will never die!'

"We were frightened. We did not want to fight him so we fled, leaving him.

"When we returned to the main war party, we kept quiet. But Wolf Mule, wounded, told what happened. All of us but Wolf Mule were severely beaten."

With his mouth Tall Bull motioned to Little Man, a short, stout warrior, seated on the other side of the fire. "Never again," Tall Bull said.

Little Man nodded.

LATER on the edge of the main camp Jeroen walked alone and Little Man approached. "White Man Running, *nih-aahtohvits!*" he said, "Listen to me! Tall Bull and the Dog Soldiers have grown strong." He placed his forearm on Jeroen's chest. "He rides on the white man even when the tribe is quiet. Will you go?"

"Yes," Jeroen said and when Little Man walked from him, he made his bed on the ground a short distance from camp and lent his eyes to the dark. His mind went to ambitious wandering. Cunning the mountain runners, swift the gold black eagle, he knew the clan, the Dog Soldiers, tribe vanguard and welfare, secretive, select. They suffered no fear. Singing their war songs, singing all night, when daylight came again they danced, the people watching, the warriors halting four times before they reached the center of the village. The extra moccasins and dried food were prepared and they would start out together the next day. Jeroen woke before sunrise, said

123

nothing to Bird In Ground or Highwalker, and left camp with the Dog Soldiers.

HE ROSE among the ranks, proving himself valuable, a man of strong deeds over the enemy, and soon he was held a little lower than the young chiefs, an honored position for a warrior. Quietly, he felt joy for life, and on each return from a raid or bloodletting he avoided Bird In Ground. The tribe looked away from this. His name among the Dog Soldiers became a good name.

With Tall Bull and Little Man he rode hard and the Dog Soldiers were joined by more young men who did not belong to the clan, but who wished to make names for themselves. Under cover of darkness and night they flew, returning only when they had counted coup and taken many scalps. They sought the life of men and word of death, and because of Tall Bull's brazenness many of the old thought he would die in battle, beckoned forth bold as old night but fragile as man. Quiet, by firelight, Little Man drew White Man Running close, motioning with his lips toward Tall Bull. "He carries only a tomahawk. Do you see?"

"No gun. No bow?" said White Man Running.

"Only the one," said Little Man, eye alight, fist in hand. "Closer to the enemy, faster to count coup. Like the Pawnee Chief." Little Man pointed to the stars. "Like the Seven Sisters. He will never die."

"So be it," said White Man Running, and putting his hand on Little Man's shoulder he said, "We will never die." His voice low, the sound of it like oil on his tongue, Jeroen felt translucent and born of night, conceived not solely of light but also darkness, a brothering he'd known for many years.

4

WITH ANIMAL-LIKE EASE his next contact with the enemy startled him.

He had ridden with the others to the big bend of the Yellowstone, hidden in the day, waiting for night to come and carry them. The river swept away south and bent into a large cutbank where it swelled and roiled before moving further on, brown as dust but glinting gold in the afternoon. A stand of spring aspen grew above the cutbank, upright and robed in silver flickered by wind. Over the long plain, purple sage put veins of off-colored ore in the pale yellow of the grass.

Past dusk he went with Tall Bull and Little Man and the Dog Soldiers to the white settlement called New Possibility, three miles downriver. Into the tiny town they passed quietly, on foot, not loud like the white man. Darkness covers the earth, he thought, and deep darkness its people. Such ease this way, Jeroen thought, death like a river and life a vessel to ferry the innocent home. He came into the white people's living spaces where they sat in wooden chairs at wood tables, or as they lay in woolen coverings on hewn log beds. With his bare hands he held the heads of those he had called his own. He heard their cries as he turned his arms and swift silence followed. He took what he wanted. Scalps first, skin shorn from the skull in rugged, aberrant strokes, the shock of hair warm in his hand like the pelt of something foreign. Shirts next, and coins, an axe with a broken handle, an iron skillet. But especially horses, a bay colored female, a wild-eyed roan, and from a wooden cross-post near the largest of the town's three houses the big black gelding he claimed for his war horse.

Out from there he rode with Tall Bull and Little Man, conquering the Crow, taking the hair of the foe, swift with the Dog Soldiers, killing the Pawnee. Some who had been Cheyenne allies, Indian, white, were enemies again. After killing, he traveled back with the others and gathered a short distance from the main camp of the Cheyenne. They burned willows and painted their faces black with powdered charcoal. They entered camp this way, as ghost men, soldiers of another world. The hair of the enemy hung from the tips of their lances. The men carried dry branches to make a tipi-shaped skunk-fire, and the warriors made themselves ready for the dance. At dark they set the skunk alight, and it made a great blaze. The entire camp was singing and dancing. Enemy scalps had been taken with no loss of life to the Cheyenne. And when again he saw his wife moving toward him from between two lodges, he noted his heart for her had opened like a great door that looked upon new country.

She looked on him gracefully. He had been to her something she had not foreseen, and she thanked the great one, Maheo.

He touched Bird In Ground's face before he turned and went with Tall Bull, walking their mounts to an old man who had a sack of medicine for horse-curing. Tall Bull's buckskin had received a lance to the flank in the last skirmish. The horse's head was low, and film covered the eyes. In the gray light the old man faced the horse east and put some of the medicine, made of small leafy plants, into his own mouth, and then came close to the horse and spit some of it into the palm of his right hand. He touched the horse's nose with it, rubbing it around the nostrils, and shook and pulled the right ear, then the left. The old man walked around the right side and spit some more medicine into his hand and shook it and rubbed it on the shoulder and then the hip, over the slant of blood on the flank, then to the shoulder and hip on the other side the same way, and back to the tail. He pulled the tail four times. The horse lifted its head and snorted.

5

JEROEN WENT from Tall Bull and brought two strong horses he'd captured to Highwalker, a big Cavalry chestnut, and a young buckskin. He placed his hand on Highwalker's chest, presenting the horses to him, and as he walked back toward his own lodge he remembered what Highwalker had told him of the first Cheyenne horses when they'd stood together over the Tongue River. White Man Running was still healing from his fight with Wolverine. "The father of all Cheyenne horses was blue," Highwalker had said. "The mare was buckskin, and from these, the elders say, every Cheyenne horse was made." Highwalker formed a fist. "Fast, loyal, strong." They stood watching the pull of water and light. Highwalker's eyes were happy. "The ones we steal..." he said, "they are only coming home."

When he approached his own lodge, Jeroen came with horses, the black and two smaller ones—a brown paint, a red horse spotted white at the rump—and walking toward the lodge, holding the simple deerskin halters of the three, an old man appeared from the dark and walked beside him a few lengths away and slightly behind. The man mumbled almost to himself, words White Man Running barely understood, of wolverines crossing mountain ranges, two animals or three, low glistening bodies bred of tooth and speed, of claw and darksome eye, hungry, finding their way. Jeroen slowed and brushed the man's shoulder and the man smiled and walked on, and when Jeroen came at last to the lodge he tied the paint and the red horse where Bird In Ground would find them in the morning.

On the willow bed she held Jeroen to her chest. She had lost all will with the massacres. Her will had been regained, she thought, in the way of their bodies in the evening.

She smiled at him as he gazed upward through the opening and saw the night black and met with stars. Multitudes, he thought, and when he slept, he dreamed. In the dream, their love could not be subdued or unmade. The spirit of the animal lived and moved and the earth buckled and rose sheer to the top of the sky where the sun made its home and ran from east to west and did not die.

6

WINTER. The horses wore the paint of the coup the Cheyenne counted. The prints of yellow hands emblazoned at shoulder, neck, and flanks. White half-moons. Red circles for bullet holes. The star-like images of blue suns. Brave Bear was the lead warrior, his body like a stone hammer, an arm drawn forth, lifted high. He wore the dog rope, a strip of buffalo hide, ornamented with feathers, threaded with porcupine quills, a slender wooden pin tied to one end—in battle he set the pin in the ground. There the Cheyenne would stand or die.

After they held the Sacred Arrows ceremony to blind the enemy, a crier gathered the warriors and Tall Bull spoke, "Our territory is vast, and it is ours to defend: from the northwest at Fat River, up Elk River and the Bighorn to Heart Mountain. From there along the Backbone of the World, down by the Medicine Wheel and through the Tetons to the south end. Then to Ghost River that empties into Infernal River, and all the way to the brown waters of the Kansas.

"Our enemies say we are the bravest warriors," Tall Bull continued. "We have no fear, they say. And so they call us crazy. We want to kill everybody. So be it. Today we kill the Pawnee."

BRAVE BEAR RODE a black paint with a white mane. The dog rope was looped over his left shoulder and worn like a banner across the chest. Together the warriors emerged from a draw and approached at full gallop over the plain, descending finally at great speed along a broken creek bed in the late dark before dawn. As they rode the world was made new and Jeroen saw in Brave Bear's face thunder on the mountain, and in Brave Bear's hair wind like a wolf nosing hunger.

They came in the half-light to touch the enemy, to kill him in his sleep. But the Pawnee were waiting and the battle erupted with sharp yells and the whistle of arrows, the lunge of spear and knife. Jeroen heard the shrieks of dying men. He saw the wide arc of club and tomahawk. So hot was the battle he felt himself burned and for a time his courage shriveled and lay down. There, silent as his war horse entered the fray he steeled his mind and drew low in the saddle. But when he saw Tall Bull knocked from his mount Jeroen's body went loose and his heart surged as if filled with a great storehouse of power that pushed him forward, leaping from his horse to join Tall Bull, rushing with the others on foot. They descended the slant of a coulee and ran up again to the top of a small knoll. Here the fighting of many warriors converged hand to hand, forming a knotted irregular line, and here an arrow flew, splitting Brave Bear through the neck, killing him instantly. The victory tilted as the warriors amassed, attacking each other, and the Cheyenne fought vigorously, forced to a standstill, torsos bent back, arms thrown to the sky.

They wavered, holding the line and just when the battle looked to sway in favor of the Pawnee, Jeroen seized the dog rope at Brave Bear's chest, freed it and thrust the pin in the ground. With a swift downward motion he snapped the lunge of a Pawnee lance, then took up the broken spear tip and pierced the chest of his attacker. Upright over the body he shouted, "*Nahih Nihohvihoo-vitsih!* Here we stand!" and when he leapt forward, the Cheyenne were all around him, screaming, felling the enemy. They advanced and as Jeroen opened his mouth in a war cry he was pounded in the skull by a Pawnee hammer. A piercing pain came, followed by a dull flood that slowed the body to nothing. He fell, effortless, almost weightless backward on the grass and saw the world spin in a slow arc as he began to lose breath. He didn't want to die lain backward on this small rise of land. His vision grew dark, narrowing. He called out. He saw the sky, grey-white and open with light. A thought came, in his mother's voice, *What is man, that Thou thinkest of him?* The heavens appeared swept bright with down-falling snow and then his eyes went dark and sleep cloaked him. Here, like the touch of a friend or the kiss of a child, he remembered a time long before, without bound or border, beneath all, before his life had seemed so strange to him. No snow, or even sky. A place barren and displaced, of dry heat and sage, of fine white dirt sifted by wind. He saw tall lodgepole pines, stripped and sword-tipped, side by side and uniform. Four high walls. A fort. A fortress. The walls fell in the four directions, and on the ground, he witnessed his body naked, face down, arms wide, alone. Pale sun. Blue sky. A slight wind in the air and the scent of water as he lay still. He heard a Cheyenne bird song, like a lark's lament. In the dream world he sat up, then stood, searching. From a stand of willows along a creek bed Bird In Ground walked toward him. She came near, as ever he had known her, hard face, soft eyes. She touched his cheek with her hand. She took his hands in hers and turned them and kissed the underside of his wrists. He heard the sound of a whirlwind. The sound came from beneath her, from the light in which she walked or from the land itself. Then she walked away from him and the sound was gone. He followed, reaching for her but when she turned to him her face was pocked with disease and he leapt back from her and fell to his knees as she vanished.

He did not wish her gone and so he yelled for her, but no answer came.

He was taken from the hill to a nearby river, the Bent Calf. He lay in a bed of mud at the riverside, touched by Tall Bull and Little Man, then each of the Dog Soldiers, prayed over, offered up, spirit and animal, and man. The Pawnee were routed; all dead, every horse taken. Borne in arms no longer foreign, laid down among fires, Jeroen slept for a night and a day. Blood seeped from a wound at the base of his skull. Body as if dead, hard and black the river of dreams, he ran on water and up mountains, across ranges of timber and exposed rock, cliff faces, slants of granite, edges of stone, over the tilted rock-blades upthrust and broken on the edge of the earth, body and hair made of soil, shaking his head he consumed the stars with his mouth, lips red and black drinking deep the black and silver sky, wanting, emptied, ravenous, shaped of need, he ran to an end of all and to the death to which he'd always felt tethered, but here now, weary, he saw light at the edge of the world and he was given back his life.

He woke, touching the wound behind his ear. He felt the raw opening, the dried blood, and bone like wood or stone. Fate, he thought. Grace. And listening he lay still. And more words came, *Put on your garments of splendor.* Old words. Words his mother had whispered, stroking his hair. A bright white moon appeared in the form of a sickle overhead, the nimbus darkly encircled—so like the evening he'd broken Wolverine's jaw and poured out the animal's life. At dawn the other warriors would drive one-hundred stolen horses south along the Bent Calf, over the high bench of the plains, back to the Cheyenne camp on the Big Bear. They had waited, ready to carry him home. But now in pitch blackness knowledge smote him. He must see her. He signed to them and walked to his horse and they followed and watched and made loud clicking sounds with their mouths and yelled courage to him: "*Eh-peh-vah!*" "*Eh-peh-vah!*"

They helped him to the back of the animal and Tall Bull slapped the animal's flank and whistled and the big horse bolted carrying Jeroen on a straight line south. Under the moon the earth was silvering and motionless. The fields lay open and lone trees stood like stark hands on the ridges north and west. Fast, he made ground, but his hands felt brittle. He feared what lay ahead. Giving the horse open rein he abandoned all and when dawn came he pressed harder, pushing through the day and again into night. He'd left his common horses behind and in the dark he came upon a sleeping camp of Crows. A ways off, he stood with the horse among jack pine and sage in a dip of land where water glistened. Black cottonwood deadfall lay next to him, huge limbs arched like the comb of a bird, teeth of Neolithic grandeur, the barrel of the tree split by lightning, burned in two, and out from the burn the grey white of sharp limbs that jutted upward clean and bare. He dismounted and hobbled the horse and said a prayer for what the horse had given. He walked through sage and blue bunchgrass, heard a whispering at the sides of his legs and thought of Bird In Ground. Touch, and the absence of touch. He walked like one invisible, direct to the lodge of a soldier chief where he took an appaloosa war horse. The animal, grey and dappled white, bore Jeroen without pause for another night, another day, and by the third eve the land lay behind.

His hope, unspoken, ahead.

7

ASPEN AND LARCH half-held with light, shadows of lodgepole pine, the night cold with stars, he walked the horse over open ground and passed into the stillness of camp. A slight wind pushed at the lodges. A few children gathered at the shoulders of the horse, touching the horse's legs and chest, the mane, their hands small and dark on the grey coat. He beheld their slender arms and gaunt faces, the closed lips and open eyes, and seeing them his shoulders felt heavy and he turned away. A path opened as he passed the lodge of Highwalker and beyond he saw his own lodge, red fire lit within, smoke lifting from the lodgepoles in the blackness. Before entering he tied the horse behind the lodge. With surety he walked to the opening and came almost silently to be inside. The circle was full and warm with fire, the smell of winter-rose and sweetgrass. An older one, Kicking Woman, knelt on the ground over his wife. Why Kicking Woman? he thought, and remembered her medicine. Strong woman. Life-bringer. He heard Bird In Ground's measured breathing. No one looked toward him.

He knelt closer, beside Kicking Woman, and when the old woman saw him she shouted, moving her hands wildly in front of her face. He spoke harshly to her, "Hush!" but the old woman's eyes appeared stricken. Do I have blood on me? he wondered. He touched at his face and neck, the back of his head behind the ear. Angrily, he motioned the woman back, and she looked straight at him and waved him away as if warding off spirits. She covered her face with one hand.

He grew still, watching.

Bird In Ground lay on her back, her head buried in skins at the outer edge of the circle, the bones of her eyes and the line of her nose tilted and lit by firelight. Quiet, he told himself. He pressed his hands to his side, wiping sweat on his leggings as he pulled at the fringe of the red war shirt Tall Bull had given him. He drew close and came to one knee and brushed back Bird In Ground's hair. Beside him, the old woman hissed. He touched his wife's forehead, calming her. He kissed her, saying, "*Nehmehohtahts,*" I love you, and when he touched her face

133

the language of his mother came to him and he called her, "*Milah-chek*." Darling.

She said nothing. She held her stomach with her fists.

She believed, then, she hated him with an ancient hatred.

"Away?" he asked, pointing to the opening, and Bird In Ground nodded.

He looked at her, then turned and left the lodge.

Outside, his clothes stuck to his body. He stared back at the opening. We give to each other, he thought, in the dark between us. And what we give no one knows. He looked at his feet. The ground shone, iridescent, glinting like metal.

He crouched and faced the lodge and gathered his knees in his arms. The air was cold. He sat for a long time, staring. He did not know if this should be his place or perhaps further on toward the river, but he remained here, silent and still. A scream came, followed by wailing. The sound hitched and rose.

In Cheyenne a voice said "The baby."

"*Mih-ishivohts?*" he whispered.

He thought to rise, but instead wrapped his knees tighter in his arms and put his head down and wept.

Standing, he entered the lodge and saw Kicking Woman seated before the fire, the child wrapped all around, tiny face pressed to the old woman's neck. Where is Bird In Ground? he thought, and finding her in shadow beyond the fire, he went to her. Kneeling, he saw that her shoulders were open, appearing nearly translucent in the firelight, a painful questioning expression on her face. He sat down next to her and drew her to him so that he cradled her body. He touched his hand to her forehead. A look of resignation, he thought, her face so drawn and smooth. Behind him the old woman went out, taking the baby. He pressed his lips to Bird In Ground's face, kissing her cheek, but she turned away and said something obscure in Cheyenne. He didn't understand her. She held her hands to her chest. He touched her shoulder.

"*Hohmivohnihnihsts!*" she said.

"Go! Be gone."

"No," he said.

"*Hohmivohnihnihsts!*" she said, viciously.

"I will stay," he whispered.

She was silent. He lay still.

Over her body he leaned and stared closely at her. Her look was unknowable and as he moved closer she turned and brought her eyes to his. In the shadow he found the deep-lined bones of her face, the upthrust of bone behind the ear, the circular bones of jaw and shoulders. Places of affection into which he might fall again. He took her hands in his and she did not repel him and he drew them to his face, and turning her hands over he kissed them. Her eyes shone as glass and he saw the animal in her, and suddenly he felt terror and lay back, breathing.

The fire burned.

Neither slept.

Up through the V of the lodge, through the crisscross of lodgepoles, black sky subdued an immensity of stars.

Far down, beneath the surface of the world, dawn.

FOURTEEN TYPES OF BELIEF

I

THE HALLS are set with grey-white tile that shines a dull light, the walls built of hard red brick. As the boy walks, the other students look at him funny. Everett Highwalker is a freshman in high school. Pimpled face. Shock of black hair. He holds his head down. Slender, he carries his basketball wherever he goes, places the ball under the chair during class, cups it like a loved one everywhere else. He is five feet seven inches tall and barely weighs one hundred pounds. He thinks of his mother, her face in her hands at the kitchen table, the slant of her shoulders.

From his own sorrow over the loss of his father he too is in great pain, but he gets taller, and as he does he works, and the school seems to grow smaller as he grows larger. Sophomore. Junior. He studies, plays, puts time in the gym, runs, shoots, lifts weights, gains strength. His face clears. He grows to six feet four, weighs 195 pounds, and starts at forward for one of the top teams in the state. His mother works long hours, holds two jobs. A velocity breathes in him and he sees how the other athletes seem to look at him as they might a lion that paces and peers. He lives in Portland, Oregon where the mouth of the Columbia opens wide and wounds the body of the ocean.

2

HIS SENIOR year he walks more upright but still he keeps his head down. When teachers ask him about last night's game he says how well his teammates played. When they ask him about his vertical, his jumper, his defense, how he won the game on a last second shot, he replies, "Still working. Need to work hard."

"Where did you learn to work like that?" asks the Vice Principle who overhears the boy in the hall and loves to talk hoops. Man with grey-black hair who said he was slender once, though he's beefy now. He played power forward for Duquesne in the late 80s. The boy holds the ball in his hands, shuffles his feet.

"My father," the boy answers, and the VP says, "How about getting some lunch?" and the boy says, "Sure," and they walk together to the cafeteria.

They find a place near the far wall.

The boy's father was half-Cheyenne, and big.

DelVon Highwalker. Husband to Maria. Father of Everett.

He loved basketball like he loved family.

"He taught you what it takes to be great, didn't he?" says the VP who looks the boy in the face. The boy says, "He did," and puts his head down and clenches his jaw to keep the tears from his eyes. "Him, and my mother." They sit at a table with benches attached by metal to the under works of the tabletop. The boy cups the ball, turns it, rolls it, considers the curve and the channels, the leather, the feel of heat in his hands.

"I want to be someone," he says. "Go somewhere."

"Somewhere?" the VP asks.

"The next level," Everett said, "not just here."

The VP sees it in the boy, but at the same time he recognizes the shape of loss in him. Most men never achieve what they hope for, the VP thought.

3

WHEN HE was young the boy's father cupped his face and said, "Focus on a target within a target. If your shot slips in and out, it's always the eyes. Lock in the eyes and that won't happen. Got it?"

"Got it," the boy repeated.

"And I got you," his father said and pulled him hard to his chest.

This, a month before his father died.

He's gone now, the boy thinks, and it eats at the edge of his mind and only fades when he works on his game. Ball fake, drive left, pull up, nothing but net. Shot fake, drive right, pull up, bank off the glass. The movements and the rhythm are his only sense of calm. When he needs to, he goes to one knee on the outdoor court at night and cries. From the next world his father welcomes his tears, the boy thinks.

He thinks his father cries too.

4

THE VP played against the boy's dad in city league, knows the boy's dad worked at the mill. He worked heavy machinery and died when the boom of a crane broke loose and crushed the man's chest.

A giant of a man, solitary in the world.

Another lunch. More talk of hoops.

The VP reaches, touches the boy's shoulder for a moment. "Your father could shoot the J," he said, "and defend like no other."

"Serious ball player," the boy says, and looks down.

"A thing of beauty, watching him play." The VP holds his own follow through in the air and smiles. "How about lunch every Wednesday?"

"Sure," the boy replies.

5

THE BOY gets offers from a few small colleges. He dreams Division I and decides to walk on at the University of Oregon in the Pacific Athletic Conference, the PAC 12, where the Wizard of Westwood, John Wooden, guided UCLA to ten national titles and four undefeated seasons. That summer, the VP invites him to play on a tour team of all-stars from the Pacific Northwest, an international travel team to Great Britain, Scotland and the Isle of Man. The VP is the coach. The boy averages 37 a game and feels unstoppable. The team goes 9 and 2 beating Wales, Liverpool and Manchester. They lose to the London Knights and the Torches of Edinburgh.

In the US, at the DI level, no one knows his name.

He walks on at Oregon and makes the team.

The coaches dog him. Run him. Yell at him. Curse him.

Though he thinks he has no chance of earning playing time he works hard and sacrifices. His hunger is strong. His love for the game is stronger.

6

HIS ENTIRE freshman year he plays a total of 22 minutes in four games. He shoots 0 for 3, gathers 2 rebounds, fouls twice, and garners 1 steal. His sophomore year, three guys get injured. He weighs 220 pounds and gets 14 minutes per game, averages 4 points, 4.5 rebounds, and 1.3 steals. He takes care of the ball. The team improves and breaks .500. Midway through the season he sweeps in from the wing for a rebound in the half-court offense. Untouched, the players part before him and he plants, launches into the sky and catches an errant shot that caroms wide of the rim. Everyone is far below him now as he tip jams, massively, over two defenders. The force of the dunk is like the barrel-swing of a sledge hammer. He lands off kilter on the floor in the middle of the pack and bounces to his feet as the crowd erupts and the sound is deafening and the air seems to compress and expand and catch flame. He looks at his hands. A red mark registers high on his wrist, like a blood wound from the rim, and his teammates mob him and holler and pound his chest.

The team talks about the dunk for weeks.

From this single event he gains the nickname Tomahawk.

The play is the first of many.

Twenty games in, the coaches tell him he has made a huge contribution to the team and they will scholarship him next year. After the season, the coaching staff confirms their promise. At home for the summer, he holds his head high and walks into the gym and tells his friends from high school. They give him five and hug him and smile wide and look at him as if he is from another, brighter world.

In the kitchen he holds his mother's hand and she smiles. "So good to have you back," she says. Her face is a sanctuary.

In the dark when she sleeps he drives her car to the outskirts of town, parks and walks the clean grass incline to where he sits beside his father's grave and tells him about the scholarship and feels his eyes well. The pine trees are like sentinels. "Mom misses you," the boy says. "I miss you." He places his hands on the ground over his father. "I need you," he says. The stars wheel overhead and he feels lost but not lost, and when he rises and walks from the cemetery he remembers the sorrow takes a long time going, and perhaps is never really gone. In his dreams his father walks with him.

The next day Everett has lunch with the VP and tells him about the scholarship, and the VP slaps him on the back, laughing. He looks him in the face and says, "Congratulations! You've worked hard for this. Keep working, son."

"I will," Everett says, and before he leaves, he looks at the VP's face and pauses. "I wouldn't be where I am without you," he says. The skin on the VP's neck turns red. The man looks at his feet and taps the boy on the shoulder a few times.

"Count on me every home game," he says.

7

MID-SUMMER before Everett returns to campus, an assistant coach calls. "Couldn't give you the scholarship," he says. "We need it for other positions."

"That's not right," the boy says softly. "You lied to me. Broke your promise."

"Happens," the assistant retorts, "get over it."

8

THE BOY does but a fire burns in him, at the dishonesty of men, men unlike his father, unlike the VP. He burns and he works. He runs and jumps and increases in power. He weighs 230 pounds now and benches 280. His vertical tops 40 inches. He dribbles all over town, the ball an extension of his body, the jumper, the follow-through, the release, the backspin a gift from his father, the loft of the arc a gift from his mother, the net like rain, the sound of the swish a music that transcends the world.

"He plays defense like an army of men," his old teachers say.

"He rebounds like a wrecking ball."

He believes what they say is true because when he defends he feels alive. And when he crashes the boards, the other players fall away like trees felled in a forest. He remembers when his father took him to the Beartooth Mountains and the boy shot his first bull elk on the pass north of Two Oceans Plateau, the animal huge and ominous in the early light, a rack of tines hung back from the head, the horns thick and pointed skyward even in death. He'd used his father's Remington .243, the stock warm against his cheek, the scope a cross-haired window, deep breath blown smooth from his lungs. He saw the animal's body collapse before he heard the rifle report. He held the legs as his father made the cut from neck to base and drew the hide away from the rib cage with clean swipes of the hunting knife so that the white inner lining shone in the half-light. His father pulled out the entrails, his arms drenched in blood to the elbows. He looked to the boy then and said, "We give this to the animals. The coyote, the crow. We bring the meat home to Mama." He went back to knife work. "My father's people went hungry. Don't forget that, son."

"I won't, Papa," he said, and saw the detail of his father's frame as he boned out the animal, cutting the joints with the bone saw, quartering the elk and removing the hooves. "You're mother's words are good to me," his father said and quoted from memory what she'd read to them the night before. "He knows what lies in the darkness and light dwells with Him." The boy nodded and peered out over the land to where the sun went down. "Spirit of the Creator," his father whispered, and stood and turned to the boy. "Treat your mother with dignity, she's like the land, like the hand of God." The boy looked into his father's eyes. "Yes, sir," he said and kneeled to help cape the animal and bag the meat. His father tied the head and horns to his own pack and had the boy help hoist the pack to his shoulders. In the last light of dusk they walked in tandem, the horns upside down above his father's back, the skull heavy, the tines arched like wings.

9

BEFORE SUMMER'S end the boy and the VP travel to Alaska to put on an assembly for a school in Seldovia where the VP's good friend is the principal. Seldovia, harbor on the edge of the ocean, town of blue water in a bowl of forest and rock surrounded by small poverty-ridden homes, smoke adrift from tight tin chimneys. Every kid in town shows, and their parents with them, so the little box gym is filled to the rafters as the VP speaks to the kids about school and leadership, about grades, and dreams. The boy comes to the microphone in a baggy sweat suit and clean white Nike Airs and speaks about life. The students are a mix of Eskimo and white, native, and northern. The people who gave them breath fill his field of vision and they are strong and good, he thinks, and he feels thankful for them, for his own family, for the VP, and for basketball. He tells the kids he believes in them. He places his hand over his chest and says God resides in the strength of their fathers and the joy of their mothers, and in the end he says, "Don't stop dreaming your dreams."

He removes his sweats and walks onto the court in a white t-shirt and black silk shorts, baggy and bordered with green and gold. The kids line up under the basket on one end and the dunk show begins. He throws himself alley-oop lob passes from half-court. He tosses the ball high and it bounces off the hardwood and lofts itself to a point far above the rim as he runs and flies and meets the ball in midair. He rises higher and hammers home one-handed tomahawks and two-handed shoulder blades, a flurry of reverses, windmills, and 360s. "Clap out the beat!" he says, and the people cheer and clap in unison to a deep drum rhythm as he puts backspin on the ball and watches it return to him before he lofts another lob from half court, rounds the turn, launches, and soars on a sideways lean with his back to the rim. Up near the rim he snatches the ball from the air and touches it to his heels, and when he smashes it behind his head he hears a loud bang. Like a shout from a rifle barrel the rim breaks free and the backboard shatters.

He lands in a rain of glass, and everyone goes silent.

Shards fan at his feet and out from him in an arc that reaches to the top of the key, and wider still and more dispersed beyond the half-court line. He sees the rim on the hardwood floor, displaced like the shed horn of an animal. He turns to the kids packed along the baseline, their eyes wide and mouths open. Finally, a skinny high schooler stands and starts clapping, then the kid shouts and lifts his hands and the others stand then and they all applaud wildly and the whole gym roars as the kids gather around Everett. They touch his hands and his arms. They pick up pieces of glass to take home. He shows them the bruises the rim has made on his wrists. He smiles directly into their eyes.

10

IN SEPTEMBER he returns to the team. He gets 22 minutes a game his junior year. He weighs in at 240 pounds and hauls rebounds like a freight train. He runs faster, jumps higher, and plays harder. He gets time, goes after every loose ball, turns the momentum of the game. "He's a beast," the head coach whispers, secretly in awe, and the boy's numbers ascend. The coaching staff again promises him a full ride. The team takes another step, battles for a top four position in the league and ends up third. They lose their first two games in the league tournament but win two in the National Invitational Tournament, the NIT, losing to Seton Hall one game before the semis and Madison Square Garden.

He meets with the coaches post season. "No scholarship," they tell him again. He puts his head in his hands. The words pierce him, circling his chest like barbed wire. "We don't have any scholarships left," the head man says, "we gave the last one to the big man from Germany. You know how much we need a big man."

That weekend he goes home. Face flushed and heart pounding he tells the VP.

They return together to meet with the coaches.

II

ROOM OF GLASS windows and leather chairs. Everyone seated. The head coach begins, and the words are smooth from his tongue but sound brittle and foolish in the air. "We've been more than fair here," he says, but already the VP has had enough. "Shut your mouth," he orders the coach, "I'll do the talking." He slams his hands on the table, stands and leans over until they are eye to eye. "You are a liar," he says. "The boy has earned every inch of ground he's gained. Treat him right." The VP's face is red, the tendons in his neck like taut wire. He turns and looks at Everett and his face softens. "He's like a son to me. Like a son to the whole town he comes from." He draws himself back and sits down again. He stares at the coach.

"You need to be a better man," he says. "This is beneath you and your program. Treat him right. He'll give you everything."

The coach's head is down now.

He looks up at the boy.

The boy stares back and does not waver.

"You want that scholarship, son?" the coach asks.

"Yes," the boy answers.

"It's yours," the coach says. "I agree. We need to treat you right."

12

AND THE COACH does.

The boy signs on the line and enters his senior year ready.

His teammates elect him team captain. He starts every game, averages 11.6 points, 12.4 rebounds, and 2.1 steals. He is named conference Defensive Player of the Year and the team advances to the championship game of the league tournament winning 92-87 in double overtime as the fans swarm the court and the players and coaches are swept up in the middle. The VP meets him near the center circle, and they embrace and streamers rain down on everyone. As the boy releases the VP, the older man wipes tears from his face and sees the boy moving with his teammates to where they bunch near the closest backboard. He watches as they climb the ladder, and after the nets are cut the VP waves to the boy and the boy smiles and waves back.

After the celebration dies down the team gathers in the locker room where the head coach holds one of the nets out to Everett and says, "To our captain." The coach places it around Everett's neck and the team roars and the point guard punches Everett's chest and yells, "For being a killer!" and the first assistant shouts, "For leading us here!" Everett bows his head and the team bumps his shoulders and starts dancing, and they dance all the way to March Madness where they ride a wave of momentum to the Sweet 16 before they are finally knocked off in Indianapolis by eventual champion Kansas.

13

WHEN THE BOY returns home, he walks to the high school early and asks the VP to breakfast. The VP gladly accepts and they walk together in the dark to a bright-windowed diner two blocks north. Midway through the meal the boy takes the net from his backpack, reaches out and places it like a necklace over the older man's head.

"For all you've given me," he says.

"It was nothing," the VP says, and his voice cracks. "Thank you, Everett."

14

WHEN BREAKFAST is done they stand. The VP grips Everett's arm. "Let's go show your father," he says, and they drive in the dark to the edge of town where they park and walk to the grave. They stand beside the headstone where the boy listens as the VP tells the story aloud and thanks Everett's father, and tells Everett's father his strength runs in his boy like lightning. When Everett and the VP go from that place the ground is firm beneath their feet. Down a slight descent their shoes make footprints in lush grass. A remnant of darkness still robes the land as they behold granite forms as if risen from the earth, crosses over apexes of stone, marble angels whose arched wings and raised swords beckon light. Everett lifts his face. Near the far wall of the graveyard the trunks of great trees pattern the earth, their limbs reaching skyward in a single sweep of motion.

"We cannot stay another year; we want to go now. Before another year has passed we may all be dead, and there will be none of us left to travel north."

—Chief Morning Star of the Cheyenne

Oklahoma, 1877

BLACK WOUND

WE ALL came from the wound.

Dry red dirt on the soles of their feet the families of the fighting Cheyenne escaped an Oklahoma prison camp in darkness. Big land, Oklahoma, and fertile as the body of a lover. But in the dawn of that age a tide of destiny was made manifest and rode west like a beast of prey, and none were safe and none secure and all were eaten, devoured, or scattered. "North, we must go north," said Chief Morning Star, also called Dull Knife, "and if we die we die north. Not here, where we die like dogs." And so Morning Star's band gathered their small number and fled under cover of night, fighting at the rearguard with pursuant Cavalry, advancing with the vanguard back to the home country. Morning Star, White Antelope, Sitting Man, Left Hand, Black Bear, and Little Finger Nail—these and their own. The women, the men, the children, the People. Their teeth dry and white, they moved fast, and water pulled at their wind-torn eyes and night went to day and day fell again to night. Farther north and farther west they met their end in an unholy place made desolate with body and blood.

Northward still, flurries of snow placed white ledges on the limbs of trees and as the band progressed the sky turned dense until land and sky were one and the edges of the world had smoothed into a blanket under which their dreams and desires slept like animals of a forgotten country, like bears under the dark of den and breath.

Split and split again, the band was small, and tracked and cornered, captured. Imprisoned a second time, the shadow of a raven's wing fell on the heads of women and men. Surrounded by sentinels at Fort Robinson, locked in, starved, the men were separated from the women, and the women, on occasion allowed to go to them. Here the women spoke bravely to their husbands, "Take your stand. Die fighting. We cannot go back. We cannot go forward. Die with dignity. We are with you. We love you forever." And Little Finger Nail answered, "Yes. I have lived enough. I am ready." And together, the men said, "If our women are willing to die with us, who is there to say no? If we are to do the deeds of men, bring us our guns." And the women smiled and in their hearts they sang the dying song, and aloud they said, "We will hide your weapons in the folds of our clothing," and under concealment of their clothing in broad daylight the women entered the internment house and brought forth pieces of the weapons, and the men assembled the weapons and stored them under a floorboard for the appointed time.

The men killed the sentinels first and took their guns. Then the Cheyenne fled until they were cornered above the Hat Creek bluffs in a gully a day's ride from the Fort. Led by Little Finger Nail, the number only 32, the people stood together and pronounced what must not be pronounced. Women and men and children braced themselves. The blue soldiers came on with vengeance in their eyes and rage in the marbled pillars of their necks.

The Cheyenne warriors raised their guns until the bullets were gone.

Then they bared their chests to the enemy.

The women stood and held their children upward.

They died together in that place.

Black wound against winter white.

In each family a story is playing itself out, and each family's story embodies its hope and despair.

—Augustus Napier

THE HUNGER, THE LIGHT

CHAPTER 1

THE FAMILY

AT DAWN it was a clear day, no wind, but by the time Hank picked the boy up from school a grey stroke of cloud met the horizon to the north. On the barren Highline of Montana they went with the windows down in the green Chevy Malibu up the highway beyond the town until the buildings faded and the scrap yard appeared on the left side of the road. Hank slowed and drove past the structure, a tall two-story rectangle with metal garage doors right of the front window. Mr. Olaf owned the place and parked a long brown Cadillac in front, chub-faced man with dark teeth and chew stains at the corners of his mouth. He slept upstairs.

Hank pulled into the dirt parking lot then around to a fenced area in back. The gate was wider than a bus, a closed ten-foot high expanse in the larger fence line. A makeshift tangle of barbed wire lined the enclosure and inside were a dozen or so burned-out cars, some on blocks, some flat on the orange steel of rusted rims. Jakob had his elbow out the window, his chin at rest on the crease of his arm. He noticed the blown windshields of the nearest two vehicles, both sedans, big American models from the 70s. A few shards of glass in the frame. He saw the dark insides, the seats perhaps, or just blank shapes of steel. At the back of the enclosure, the sun flashed from the roof of an angular storage shed made of sheet metal.

Jakob was bored so he thought of guitar rhythms, hand heel to mute the strings, clicking out one-twos, ta-tat-tats, with a wood slap every fourth beat. He pushed the rhythm with his fingers on the dash. He was small, but music, unlike sports, didn't ask his height. A freshman in high school, five-foot two inches tall, Nordic looking with shoulder-length dirty blond hair, he weighed ninety pounds.

In front of the gate Hank put the car in Park and revved the engine.

Jakob looked at him.

"Watch," Hank grunted.

Hank chewed the inside of his cheek. Imbecile, Jakob thought. Around his mom he called Hank, "Pops," but from day one Hank received it without acknowledgement, expressionless as a slab of concrete. Jakob had thought of calling him Bull, he nicknamed all her men, but he'd settled on Heifer, preferring to see Hank as a dense-headed cow that ate fields to the nub, dull-eyed chewing his cud, leaving a trail of excrement ankle-deep. Later when Jakob found the word 'heifer' in a dictionary during English class he put the book to his mouth and laughed out loud.

"There," said Hank, pointing to movement at the storage shed.

Two dogs emerged, big males of some strange Doberman-Rottweiler mix. Jakob heard them too, and he pushed himself back in the seat, the dogs on a dead run, a roar more metallic than animal from their mouths, like a train, he thought, or like the jets that flew from the Air Force base at Glasgow. Barking, they ran for the gate and launched, rapping their snouts into the metal's diamond pattern, standing back, growling. Their jaws made a ridiculous racket, Jakob thought, as he pressed his head back into the headrest.

He had a great fear of dogs.

These two were higher than his waist. Probably closer to his chest, he thought. The Doberman was in the legs mainly, but the rest was Rottweiler, thick bodied, block-headed.

"Come with me," Hank said and took Jakob by the wrist, jerking him across the seat and out the driver's side door. Jakob held back but Hank pushed him forward, taking him by the shoulders and positioning him before the gate not three feet from the dogs. Jakob felt strengthless and loathed himself. The near one had a ragged left ear, the flap almost entirely missing, just a crownlike edge to it. He smelled dirt and car oil, tangy body odor, the scent of alcohol from the pores of Hank's body. Jakob's eyes felt raw. He tasted, more than he smelled, Hank's breath, dank and sulfurous, heavy, overpowering. It was something Jakob's mother pointed out about Hank, sometimes publicly.

"Your breath smells like feces," she'd say, and Hank would eye her like murder.

The dog's teeth clicked as the jaws snapped. Their harsh, hollow breaths rose from deep in the chest. They want to eat me, Jakob thought. Behind him, Hank's jaw popped as he chewed his cheek, which meant the Heifer was excited and needed more snuice. Despite Hank's breath and the weight of his hands, for a moment Jakob almost felt ready for what might come.

"Watch this," Hank said loudly.

Then Hank hollered, "Down pigs!"

The dogs fell prostrate, faces on forepaws, bodies flat. Everything was quiet but for the hum of the electric lines, and the flight of a grasshopper in the scrub grass along the fence.

"Up!" Hank said, and the dogs jumped up, bellowing, lunging again.

"Pretty cool, huh?" Hank shouted in Jakob's ear, and Jakob had the odd feeling of being close to Hank.

"Power," Hank said.

Hank's voice sounded distorted so near the boy's face, and Jakob noticed the lock then, a master lock almost directly in front of him, shiny silver with a round black face. Small white numbers. Smaller white notches.

Shouting again, Hank said, "Back pigs."

The dogs shut up and trotted back through the husked-out cars. They were high-chested animals, barrel-shaped with large stonelike heads. Like warlords, thought Jakob. Like wolves.

Hank retrieved a white sheet of paper from the car. "Gotta get my time slip to Olaf," he said. He motioned toward the office with his chin.

Jakob sat on his heels and eyed the fence. Heifer, he thought. Mean as a boar. With the mind of an idiot. He heard Hank from the front of the building, overly loud, glad-handing with Olaf.

Jakob stood and took the lock in his hands. In front, the two men belly-laughed in unison. In the scrap yard all was quiet. He held the lock, his fingers on the bright silver casing.

Then he went back to the car and sat in the driver's seat with his hands on the wheel. Heifer, he thought again... power. Power of the cow, maybe. On the radio he found Foreigner, with Lou Gramm's high-edged vocals. A song called Emergency. In the ashtray he fond a scrap of paper, the numbers 20-42-12 in blue ink. He took the paper with him and got out again and approached the fence. He held the lock face, cleared it and cycled the numbers—20 right, left two times around to 42, back right to 12. When he pulled down, it popped like a knuckle. He expected noise from the back of the enclosure but none came. Quietly he slipped the lock's metal loop free, pulled the handle up and drew the gate an inch or two open. He moved the handle back down and set the lock back in place, leaving the gate unlocked and slightly ajar. He pressed the lock together again.

He went back and sat in the car.

Perfect, he thought, the gate looks closed.

CHAPTER 2

THE FAMILY BENT

IN THE CREASE between the dash and the windshield a half-eaten bag of pistachios was pressed betwen the blackened remnants of old t-shirt sleeves and an unwrapped Twinkie on a square of white cardboard. As Hank returned, Jakob stared at him in the rearview mirror. Never much for cleanliness, thought Jakob. Old goat parted his hair in the middle so it hung limp to each side, black as coal above an overgrown beard. His eyes were down as he plodded toward the car. Jakob chalked up against him his obesity, his head hooded by hair, his greasy bloated face. Jakob hated him.

"Glad I showed you those dogs?" Hank said as he got in.

"Not really," said Jakob.

Jakob knew the Heifer was trying to be nice, but Jakob wasn't interested. Hank didn't notice the lock, just looked over his shoulder and backed the Malibu out.

"Thought you had to work," said Jakob.

Hank looked at him, detected Jakob's sullenness, and shouted, "Sometimes I do, sometimes I don't."

Jakob glared.

Hank backed the car into the street, stopped, jammed the works into drive and turned toward town. He drove with his left hand and with his right he reached out and clutched Jakob's chin, and pushed the boy's face in the opposite direction. "Look that way," he said. "I don't like your face."

Staring out at the fields Jakob knew why he had opened the gate. He wanted the dogs to be free, not walled-in or chained to something ugly like he was. And he hoped someone would get hurt, a thought he had often but rarely had the courage to act on, unless it was to harm himself—he bit his nails to the quick, in the mirror he pinched the blackheads from his face like his fingers were bolt cutters. He despised school, and last year there was the mess with Pat Stone in another no-name city like this one. City of hunger. City of light. Lines from a song he'd written. And people, he thought, like cities themselves.

Jakob rolled his window up to cut the dust as Hank drew the Malibu into a circle of dirt on the side of the highway. If someone got hurt, Jakob hoped it would be Hank. The Golden Spur stood angular with a low roof, painted brown, a structure wholly unelectrified, nondescript even in daylight, narrow dark windows either side of the door. Hank made Jakob wait in the car while he went inside, played Keno and drank beer. A dog to his own vomit, he thought—a line he'd stolen from the biology teacher, Ms. Pelter, a man-like woman who wore spiders encased in glass around her neck. Jakob wedged his head between the shoulder of the seat and the vinyl bumper of the door. He pictured the dogs attacking the Heifer, ribboning him. He was stuck again, controlled by Hank's agenda, and so he thought, as usual, about guitars—this time about owning his own. The band teacher, Mr. Mason, had the guitar Jakob wanted, a clean Gibson Signature Jakob coveted incessantly: Sitka spruce surface, maple on the back and sides, 11 mother of pearl stars on an Indian rosewood fingerboard and headstock. A rhythm guitar, Mason had told him, first created for the Everly Brothers in the mini jumbo style set with double pick guards. Straight from the factory in Kalamazoo, Michigan in 1971 and then through two previous owners before Mason got it. Mason was a self-proclaimed guitar aficionado and whenever he played a solo during class he liked to call himself, "The Unacknowledged Axeman of Montana." He was bald and kept a soul patch like a dime of grey under his lower lip. He liked to pull out his Strat and lay down some Stevie Ray

Vaughn, or Hendrix, Zeppelin, or Van Halen's *Eruption.* Said he hated to part with the Gibson. It was one of seven guitars he owned. "One too many though," he told the class, on account of his newborn son.

"Two hundred and twenty-five bucks," he said. "Won't find anything like it for that price."

It wasn't too far away, Jakob thought, if he could just bide his time. He'd been lifting money from Hank's pants pockets from where they hung over the chair in his mom's bedroom. Hank passed out in his mom's bed. Jakob hated this town, the eleventh of his life if his mom's calculations were correct, excluding stints of one or two months, summers, when she'd worked construction. Baronville, it was called, northern oil outpost on the Montana/Canada border. A sign on the highway said Edward Baron struck oil in the late 1800's and made ten thousand dollars. Hank took them here for a supposed job that would get the family back on track after Jakob had "publicly humiliated" the family. Auto mechanic or pipe checker or line worker or some other dumb thing, who knew, thought Jakob. Another move, the third in less than two years, and nothing changed. Jakob knew no one and no one knew him. Except if he counted deaf Mr. Elhaven two doors down with the fenced backyard, or crazy Binder next door, the middle-aged ex-military man with the jarhead crew cut.

Jakob's mom had met Elhaven at the store and pointed the old man out once on the street. "Be nice to him," she'd whispered. "He's deaf." Jakob shook the man's hand, noticed the grey velcro-stripped tennis shoes he wore, saw kindness in his eyes. But Binder, Jakob had run from when the lunatic threatened him with a shotgun. The man stood in his clean-cut backyard, green square of grass with no fence, screaming at Jakob to stay off his property. He hadn't even been on Binder's property. Only walking the alley, making his way home.

IN THE SLANT of late sun Jakob felt the dull pressure of the door on the frontal bone of his forehead. Hank had no care for how long he made him wait. Jakob remembered their first year together, Hank's and his mom's, and how he'd lie in the narrow hall outside their bedroom door, late at night or in the early morning. Hank would step over him on the way to the kitchen for alcohol or to the bathroom to pee and Jakob would reach up and touch the man's ankle and Hank would grunt or say nothing. At some point Jakob had stopped doing that.

He sat up in the car seat and looked out above the straight edge of the bar. In the depths behind the building the sky had narrowed, darkening toward night and a gathering storm. He *had* to get out, he told himself. He just needed a way. He wished he could sing, stand with a fist in the air and pipe lead vocals for a real band. He looked in the rearview mirror. He had the face for it, a pretty face he thought, like a rich boy's face. He slumped back in the seat, convinced lead was not possible, it being too up front and requiring more than he had. But guitar, rhythm guitar preferably, not lead singer, not even lead guitar, though Mason told him his scales were dialed in, even said Jakob, "broke off difficult riffs smooth as butter." No... two steps back from the front, he could do that. And write songs. He looked out the window. It'd be a pretty penny to get that guitar. Pretty Boy, they'd call him, and he'd like it. Pretty Boy punching the rhythms on the Gibson Signature. He'd find the money, make the purchase, and be gone.

Hank walked from the bar, his face full and red, his neck purple.

The two drove home in silence.

LATE NIGHT, the silence gone, Hank and Jakob's mom stood face to face downstairs, carving into each other with their words.

"I hate you," she said.

"Shut your hole," Hank said. "You think I like you?"

Upstairs in his bedroom, Jakob picked his pencil off the floor, sat down at his makeshift desk, fiberboard table, wood stump chair, and hastily sketched another guitar, a Flying V this time. It was 11:47 pm. A table Hank had claimed from the dump. He gripped the upper portion of the table legs where they swelled like tiny, elongated calf muscles, and twisted them slightly so a birdlike sound eked from the leg holes. He'd gotten Hank to curse him this way a few nights back. His efforts brought nothing tonight.

He rose and left his room, slamming the door as hard as he could. He walked downstairs and passed through the living room. He walked into the kitchen and stopped where the counter armed out from the wall and squared off the room. Jakob's mom and Hank were in that small space, yelling. Beyond them was a thin card table up against the wall and three high-backed chairs tucked in, the upholstery white vinyl with big orange daisies. He stood between his mom and Hank and put his hands up, one in each of their faces.

"Stop!" he said.

Immediately his mom turned, shouting at him: "Not now, Everett!"

Spittle sprayed from her mouth.

He'd thought he was defending her.

"Bastard!" Hank added and clenched Jakob's neck with one hand. His mother dug her nails into the back of Jakob's arm.

"Get your ass out of this kitchen," Hank said, raising his hand to strike, but instead of slapping him, he shoved him so hard Jakob stumbled from the kitchen to the living room, tripping over the line of carpet that met the linoleum.

Jakob's face flushed. His heart felt hot. Head down, back to his mother and Hank, he eyed the undone laces of his Pro-Keds. Shoes bought for a quarter at a garage sale in Glendive, gift from the Heifer. Yellow suede, two-sizes too big. He rose and went upstairs.

In the kitchen the two were shouting at each other again.

She called him lazy asshole. He called her whore.

Back in his bedroom Jakob sat on the floor. The carpet smelled of cat urine.

He looked at his hands. Small hands, but quick, he thought. Quick fingers for chord changes, picking patterns, strum patterns, solos he'd fought to learn... he wanted to be good, real good... he wanted to give people tight slick licks the likes of which the world had never known. He frowned. Pipedream, he told himself.

CHAPTER 3

THE FAMILY BROKEN

JAKOB TAKES the pick from his back jeans pocket, grabs the band room loaner guitar, plain low-level acoustic, and turns a three-minute riff that makes his head sweat. Like death, he thinks, or death like that—made of absorption and fire, something to be lost in, like wilderness, like rage. He props the guitar against the arm of the couch and sits back. He sighs and wants to cry but won't let himself. Placing the pick in his mouth, he feels his face. He lets his mind think of a woman loving him, finding him attractive. His nose like a blade, his lips small and red. I won't need a voice, he thinks, just a face— good lines and clear skin, no marks. According to the picture his mom carried hidden in a slot in her wallet it is the one real thing his biological father gave him: a nice face, few blemishes.

He pictures how a woman might touch his face, a woman who has seen him play. She'd touch him not for sex, though he wouldn't stop her, but for understanding: to know him more, to be closer to him. He takes the pick from his mouth and smooths it between his thumb and forefinger and puts it back in his mouth.

He covers his ears. They keep yelling.

BARONVILLE. Embarrassment blew them east along the Highline due to the pact Jakob made with Pat Stone back in Havre. They'd agreed, he and Pat, to set fire to the school. The detail is what he remembers, simple print on matching blank chord charts:

Let's do it today.

A victory, he thinks now, though it went nowhere. Lunch break. Because of the gasoline, the fire burned his teacher's desk near to the ground, but nothing else caught. Tile floors. Concrete walls. He and Pat were arrested and spent two days in jail and in less than a week the Heifer relocated the family, first to Geffin, bald spot in north central Montana, then to Three Horse, uglified reservation town past Wolf Point, and finally further east to Baronville.

"No more stupid black clothes," was all the Heifer said.

UGLY, ALTERED tones from the kitchen.

So-called mom and dad, Jakob thinks, anathema.

She curses. He slams the door.

She yells at him through the door.

His hard-barking baritone, "Shut up or I'll shut you up."

Silence.

Jakob leans back and hears the wind, a north wind against which the house seems to brace itself. A few ticks at the window, the touch of a tree, the beginnings of rain. He cups his face in his hands. He can't recall the last time his mother touched his face.

The Heifer, he thinks, doesn't touch at all.

Or touches with hands hard as rock.

The yelling starts up again.

Jakob stands and wipes his hands on his jeans.

He removes the guitar pick from his mouth, fingers the clear brown-gold, the rounded edges. He holds it over his head and stares through the small translucent window up at the light. He slips the pick into the right back-pocket of his jeans. His faded black sweat-top lies in the corner of the room, arms splayed, midsection bent in on itself. He takes it up, puts it on, walks down the stairs and out the front door.

THE NIGHT is darker than he imagined, a plank of concrete like a grey arm in the yard. He leaps down the steps and sprints, jumping the sidewalk, angling toward the highway. He doesn't know where he'll go and doesn't care. A low ceiling of cloud blackens the sky. A drizzle of rain meets his face. He runs hard down the middle of the pavement and meets no cars and sees no one walking. His eyes burn and he cries.

They live in government housing a mile from town, where small squarish houses stand down from Highway 2 on straight lines to the south. They end on fields alternately fallow or brimming gold with wheat, fields he hates, fields quilting the earth from here to middle America. The old streetlamps emanate a dull orange glow, their luminous spheres attached to short metal arms atop half-cut wood-tarred utility poles—dim halos domelike over the sidewalk. Rain enters the outer rim of light, down in quick jettisons that shine on the ground. Up ahead he sees the otherworldly elongated metal of the highway lights, spidery above the asphalt.

He runs angry, with no plan but to keep running.

Every house is dark, the tall grass slicked with rain. He feels strong, cruising, floating, only slightly cold in the upper body. From up ahead he hears the noise of a semi as it descends the downgrade toward town. He stops at the highway and lets the force of the huge machine, burdened with downshifting, pass him by. A dirty mist sweeps over him and the white trailer fades east into the city. He walks to the middle of the road, turns, and follows the truck.

He keeps running, and drifts some, feeling the down slant of the asphalt, drawing himself back. His ears ring. His nose runs. The road, a two-lane hump-backed straightaway, slits the city east to west. Railroad tracks line the far side, through town and further to all the other stops on the Highline—Glasgow, Wolf Point, Poplar, through the Dakotas to Minnesota, to Minneapolis, and St. Paul. His shoes are old. He thinks of two words: Mom, Hank. Words he rarely speaks in kindness. His reedy mother, tiny, full of barbs. His step-animal, the Heifer, a fat man with vacant violent eyes.

Running, he feels nothing.

A mile or so ahead he sees the lights of the city, a faint red hue on the black underbelly of clouds, and closer the small round headlights of an oncoming car. As the vehicle approaches he moves into the car's lane. The car slows, the driver pumps the high beams. Light consumes Jakob's body. He feels ghostly and bright-headed. He runs toward the dark windshield but the car veers and takes the shoulder, lurching, kicking up stones. A loud honk blares as an old man's face appears, loose-skinned, contorted. Jakob hears a hoarse angry yell, then nothing.

Darkness.

His upper body is hot, his fists icy and hard.

He keeps running.

CHAPTER 4

THE FAMILY LOST

THE RAIN thrums the back of his head. The wind is a loud hush from the north. He considers lying down. Between the big cone-shaped beams of the highway lights lie huge fields of darkness. Dark, he thinks, deep dark. Dark, the absence of light. The highway lights are modern giants compared to the dwarfs that line his small subdivision. They spill bone-white light into the night, and he stares at their long gray necks, ultra-high luminaries erected on thin silver poles, slanted at the tip. The lights reach up, out over the road. Above them, the sky is so black looking into it he feels blind.

People don't know me, he thinks. No one knows me.

Lightning flashes and for a moment the world opens wide. Houses become vivid behind him, pale shapes in orderly lines. Then blackness swallows everything and thunder booms. He is left with an image in his mind of houses like the narrow elongated bones of forearms or thick-set femurs, the earth around them a grey-white skin that has sloughed off. In the bang of sound he doesn't flinch or grow afraid. He slows to a walk, down the double yellow line. A monumental apathy fills him. He decides to stop.

He believes if he lies down, the pavement will be hard but good, beaten down, and restful. He won't hear the cars, the rancher's trucks with their loud mufflers, the wide holler of gears from the 18-wheelers. He'll sleep and forget everything.

As he bends down and touches the road with his left hand, something far ahead catches his eye.

ALMOST BEYOND vision two forms pass into a broad circle of light. He knows they are dogs, the dogs he himself released, bodies tall and wolf-like, but more muscular than wolves. They walk, then begin running toward him. He stands upright, head high, watching until they pass again into the dark. His mouth tastes like metal. He smells asphalt, dirt and the oil ground into it, the rubber of tires, the tar of road crews, gasoline. He hears electricity in the sky, the sweep of lightning flashes and the deep stillness that harbors thunder. He hears the quick rhythm of the dogs paws on the pavement far away.

The dogs come visible again under another highway light, nearer, five lights ahead now, perhaps five or six-hundred yards. That far away they look sleek and fast. Because they shimmer, they don't look real. His shoes feel heavy as stones. He touches at the outside seams of his jeans.

From the black of Canada and the boundary lands, the north wind rises, and with it the rain comes harder. The dogs enter the darkness again. He knows he should go back to the house; he receives this thought like a strange almost unwanted salvation. But he doesn't move. He keeps staring into the dark. He should go, he tells himself, *right now*. Closer still, the animals emerge. He sees the pink ribbon of their tongues at the side of their mouths as they run. Dobermans, he thinks. Rottweilers.

The words jolt him and he flies.

The dogs move with their heads down and Jakob lowers his head too, running wild, pumping his fists. But his shoes are almost black now, waterlogged, banging at the road. Behind him the dogs claw the street and when he looks again, lightning flashes, showing their stark faces, the strange ear of the lead dog, truncated, half-eaten. The sky goes dark and Jakob enters the glow of another circle spread wide on the highway. He is halfway across, frantically looking back when they enter the edge of the light one light behind him. He turns, runs to the first house and leaps a small picket fence. K Street: one over from his own. No pavement, just gravel.

I can make it, he thinks.

Across the front yard, along a narrow path at the side of the house, he moves quickly, bumping his shoulder once on the wall. The path opens on a wide backyard picketed like the front. At the far end of the yard he barely clears the fence before turning up the alley.

A minute later he hears the dogs in the gravel, fighting to make the corner. At a house on the left he grips the top of a short chain link fence and hurls himself over. Landing, he falls to his knees and scrambles up. The dogs rise behind him, clutching the fence top, wriggling into the yard. He reaches a gate, unlatches it and slams it behind him. He runs beside the house and comes out onto his own street. His house is at the far end. He runs harder and cusses and starts crying again.

For a moment he hears nothing, just his own rants and hard breathing. He wants to panic. He calms himself. The gate was topped by a curved metal swirl, a length higher than the rest of the fence. High enough, he thinks. He slows. Faintly in the distance he hears snarls and the snapping of jaws as the dogs bang their faces into the gate. Volumes louder the storm surges to an ultimate build, factories of noise in the industry of night. The rain has torn a hole in everything. Silver and black. Water. Sky. All is nothing, he thinks. He arcs into the street and runs straight ahead and the voice of the dogs dies on the howling wind.

Laboring, he holds his side and slows to a jog.

For a few seconds the wind calms and he hears a bright sound, high, pronounced. A sound of familiarity and conviction. He pictures the latch on the gate, lifted by the nose of one of them. He pictures the mouth of the lead dog carving

169

flesh from his wrist, jaws hinging open and shut, splintering bone.

When he turns he finds the dogs in the street, running straight for him.

He bolts for Mr. Elhaven's place, the tall fence, a backyard he can rely on, two down from his own. The dogs gain on him as he feints to the side of Elhaven's, to the back where he gathers and catapults himself, slamming bodily some feet up the giant chain link fence, gripping the small metal squares, climbing. Pain registers in his hands as he reaches the top, swings his leg over and drops. He lets out a small uncontrolled yelp before rolling sideways on the flooded grass of the backyard. He turns and sits on his haunches and breathes. I'm safe now, he thinks, and when the dogs arrive, he eyes them and gloats. "Pigs," he says. "You won't get over that."

He blows heat into his hands.

Heads down and teeth chalk white, the dogs bellow like forges, bodies black and slick in the rain. He finds them beautiful. They leap. The fence repels them.

Lightning fractures the sky and the night births thunder, mythic sounds as of mountains falling or earth opening, and for a span all is blind and all is changed. In the space between the houses, on the horizon to the north a diadem of light branches upward from the surface of the world. Then a great booming, and more blackness, and the sky alight again, cracked with crooked forks of light, the edge-burn hot and clean.

He sits on his heels, clutching his knees to his chest. Rain pummels him.

He is alone in a wide puddle of water that covers nearly the whole expanse of Elhaven's back yard. Like toy battering rams the dogs keep jumping at the fence, growling, snapping their jaws.

"Wear yourselves out," he says and he gets up and walks closer.

At the top of his lungs he yells, "Down!"

"Back!" he screams.

The dogs hit the fence with their heads, bloodying their flat, short faces.

He has no power over them.

They're done, he thinks, tears on his face, they're cooked. But they keep on.

In among the facial bones, in the dogs' wide, thick skulls, the thin slits of their eyes appear buried and narrow. Sitting again, holding his knees in his arms, he puts his head down and waits. But no one comes.

"Go ahead," he yells again. "Knock your heads in."

He likes the heart they have, the appetite, even with him secure behind the fence. "I'm safe," he says aloud, and he feels puffed up, as big as he wants to be, followed by the certainty that he is actually small, the same nothing he's always been, pale and wet in this puddle, full of fear. He is more afraid than ever.

He wraps his knees tighter in his arms and considers killing the dogs, but has no idea how he might do so, frail as he is, and without a weapon. He looks around, hoping to find a hard-edged implement or bludgeon, a broom handle or two-by-four, a baseball bat. He finds nothing. In the far corner of the yard is Mr. Elhaven's tool shed, square of tin in an ocean of broken black water, the water beaten to pieces by the rain. The world harbors rage, he thinks. A silver master lock with a black face seals two white tin doors.

He decides to wake Elhaven but as he approaches the back door of the house the ragged-eared dog trots down the fence-line, slips his snout under the latch of the gate there and enters the backyard. I'm dead, Jakob thinks, and wishes, painfully, he would have noticed that gate. The dogs flow into the yard like eels as Jakob breaks for the back fence, splashing wide holes in the water's surface. The dogs are fast, their angle precise.

The lead dog overtakes him as he reaches the fence.

A scream unhinges from Jakob's throat.

CHAPTER 5

THE FAMILY

NO LIGHT and no one stirs. Jakob's momentum carries him forward and he scrambles up the fence, dragging the dog as it jerks convulsively, jaws locked on a bell of denim at the bottom of his right pant leg. The second dog half-climbs the flanks and head of the first but fails to gain purchase, careens and hits the fence left of Jakob.

In a vigorous thrust Jakob moves to the top, makes a quick reach, finds the crossbar and secures a handhold. He hoists his chest upward and throws his arm out, checking another lunge from the second dog, but the dog bites his forearm, tearing a wide hole in his sweatshirt before falling back to the ground. A crescent of blood opens on Jakob's skin and he sees the bite-flap raised and half-mooned before the blood wells and branches down his arm. He pulls himself up, trying to dislodge the animal on his pant leg. His jeans are tight to his hips, the dog flailing below, heavy as a hay bale. He strains upward feeling the pull of tension in the dog's mouth. The stitching creaks and finally the material shears as the dog rips the denim free and falls, white-eyed, smacking its head and chest on the ground and letting out a single yelp.

The second dog sniffs the lead dog as Jakob draws himself to the fence-top and throws his leg over. He sees his shinbone white as snow in the ragged hole. He pushes his body over the top and the sudden imbalance flings him free as he floats in mid-air, his mind like a lost thing until he lands flat on his back in the alley.

As if he's swallowed a stone he lies holding his stomach. Both dogs are on the other side of the fence, an arm's length from his face as they paw vigorously and splash muck and water behind them. Jakob can't find air. He gags. He lets out a thin groan. Then his chest opens and he sucks in whole breaths, arms wide, legs straight, rain hard on his face. Grit covers his teeth. His hair is set back from his head, starlike, the locks spread and dirty in the gravel.

I've done it, he thinks, I've won.

His house is only two doors down now, two sets of garbage cans, then his own weedy back yard, his own back door. Beyond the house lies the big field, and beyond the field, darkness, and in the darkness a flash, the horizon lit from below as if by fire, a solitary line of light beneath the storm.

He rises, and when he does the dogs leave the fence and run back for the open gate. He knows undeniably they will circle in front of Elhaven's. Try to head him off on the far side of Binder's lawn, the lawn mown tight to the wall of weeds that delineates the beginning of Jakob's backyard. He needs to beat them there. Ahead, he sees the dented metal of Hank's garbage cans in their rotted wood frame.

Running, his eyes wildly search the line of weeds between his house and Binder's but before he gets there the dogs emerge low and quick, and Jakob ducks behind Binder's tall silver trash cans. A dream, he thinks. The sleek fur of their bodies oiled as a raven's wing. Their solid, blood-stained noses and the silken complexion of the face and neck. The dogs sweep into his yard and disappear into the height of weeds.

From behind the cans, he watches. The lids are chained shut. Binder's jarhead ways. The weeds are knee-high and wet from the torrent of rain and beyond them he sees the emptiness of the big field and out far, darkness where there was light. He places his hand on the back of his neck. His skin is wet and cold. Rain strikes his chest. He imagines Binder the military man, Montana militia, sees him in a shooting stance on the back step, shotgun a double-barreled canon that blows the dogs away.

Think, he tells himself, as the lead dog comes out of the weeds and sniffs the ground on the line between Binder's yard and his. For a moment at least, they've lost him. Downwind, he thinks. When he looks again the lead dog is on the small slab of cement at the back of Jakob's house. Nose down, the animal paces back and forth in front of a tall metal-framed screen door. The wood door beyond it is open, a thing Jakob's mother does to let the heat out when it's too muggy.

Jakob moves into the gap and enters the yard on a dead run.

The lead dog turns, facing him.

The second dog trots in from behind and Jakob goes stock still.

Corner of the eye, speed like mercury, the dogs converge, running for him.

Jakob tastes bile in the back of his throat. He wants to flee. He wants a gun. He wants to maim these dogs, kill them. He lowers his head and runs for the screen door.

The lead dog moves straight on and Jakob runs at him, seeing the dog's ear, the nakedness of it. Jakob doesn't dodge or look away even as the dog leaps with such force the impact snaps Jakob's head back and torques his body sideways. The bite carves an opening in Jakob's face from the upper right side of his forehead, across his nose in an S, all the way to the underside of the jawbone. He bends and falls, throwing his forearm, flipping the dog crazily behind him. The second dog's teeth puncture Jakob's calf but he recoils and rolls and in one flawless motion throws the dog aside, rising as he runs and jumps for the screen and breaks through. His cheekbone and hip meet the vinyl floor where he slides and comes to a stop. He scrambles up and throws the door shut.

Head down, he breathes.

He listens to the dogs beyond the door, tearing at each other, clawing the metal.

Blood spills from his face and pools on the floor.

He sets the deadbolt and looks through the small square-shaped window in the upper portion of the door, watching the dogs leap up. They sense him as they bump the window with their mouths, bloodying it. Madness, he thinks. He fears they might break through despite the height and firmness and smallness of the window. He moves to the sink and touches the edges of the wound in his face. He stands for a long time with his hands at the sink watching the blood slip from his chin into the basin.

In the small chamber of the laundry room sounds are muffled, the bump of the dogs' heads on the outside, the grind of their mouths gnashing, the bigger sound of the storm. He stands over the sink for a long time, hearing nothing from his mother, or from Hank. Finally, he turns and when the far wall touches his shoulder he slides to the floor, sets his feet out before him and sits in the semi-dark as the blood drips from his chin to his sweatshirt and blackens a circle wider than a fist. Blood warms the underside of his pant leg. His calf aches. He stares blankly ahead. Strands of his hair stick to his neck. He fumbles in his back jeans pocket, finds the pick, amber triangular disk, lovely, he thinks, iridescent even in the dark. When he sets it on his tongue and closes his lips his mouth feels comforted. His mind is light. He sits still and it seems to him all the blood is running slowly out of him. He thinks he should drink something.

He is too tired to lift himself.

Far on, the light of morning wakes him.

The dogs are quiet. There is no rain. A shaft of sun from the window places the bright gold shape of a diamond on his chest. He feels warm. His eyes burn. When he stands he hears movement outside. Light-headed, he flips the pick with his tongue, moving it to his cheek. His mouth waters. He looks out the window, watching the dogs stretch and stare up at him. He hadn't noticed it before, the faint brown mask on each face in the shape of a butterfly. The dogs turn and disappear into the weeds before they reappear on the lawn at the back of Binder's yard. They cross the alley, heads high, lips still quiet with sleep. Their faces dark and indistinct, they slip into the corridor between two houses.

They're gone, he thinks.

Taking off his shoes and socks he walks from the room. His feet dampen the floor. The sun from the front room lights his whole body.

He will walk from his wounds, he thinks. Be a man. Abandon this place.

He will abandon. He will be abandoned.

Through the hall he sees the blue-white glow of the television and the couch where his mother lies sleeping. She has her back to him, a small baby-blue pillow tucked beneath her head. He witnesses the slight curve of her body, her tiny feet at rest on Hank's lap. Hank's head is tipped back, the drone of his snore discordant with the smooth hush of the television. Tenderly, Hank holds her feet in his hands.

SMOKE

Love is a smoke made with the fume of sighs.

—Shakespeare

—for Jonathan Takes Enemy and Charlie Calf Robe

THE WORLD CLEAN AND BRIGHT

A TRIPTYCH

A nation is not conquered until the hearts of its women are on the ground. Then it is done, no matter how brave its warriors or strong its weapons.

—Cheyenne Proverb

I

HER DAUGHTERS

THE WORLD clean and bright, long healed of ash and fire, metal, dust, and chips of bone, here among the world remade, the shadow of the former age. River Bird, intelligent in the ways of men, young medicine woman, warrior, walked the tree line on the slope of the mountain her people called High Hat.

Below, she saw the long line of the river White-Stones-Moving bent west along the shade of a cutbank, dark blue arc of shadows and out again, slaked with sun, arm of light to the edge of the earth. She walked and gathered curt herb and tart root and by nightfall she returned to mix the herbs with bird bread from her pouch, spit in her hand, form a paste, and layer the paste on the eyes of her sister, Dark Eye, the second born, hoping to heal the child of blindness. In the mountains to the south, she saw fire on a slow burn, taking a large body of land, and she watched for a while, the fire rifting, raging like a face of hatred, holy in the deep dark. She felt rain on her face, rain like a river, and saw in the distance a great bulk of smoke rising.

Night fell and blindness cloaked all, and over the People, the Sichsayas, the moon rose and the earth moved to obscure the sun, and in the hearts of men a fervor gestated, born of that which conceals and hides and makes its way as of the owl or the snake, in silence, unwanted, deadly.

WHEN THE CHILD Dark Eye grew older she walked with River Bird in the evening of her youth, nine summers Dark Eye's given age, the two singing the Sichsayas songs, the healing song, the light song, the song of mourning, the song of death. And Dark Eye remained mostly blind but because of River Bird, she saw color, and felt and tasted texture with her hands, and with River Bird she smiled, for they stayed close as they walked, and with River Bird the world did not reach to hurt her. Moving together, singing, they gathered berries, the green berry shehshehvoh, the blood berry chokecherry. They walked filling a broad-pouch to bring back to camp and prepare the fish speared that day.

FROM HIS PLACE in a narrow cave on a high cliff above the wood Heavy Head the Lost One overheard slight strains of song, and listening, at last, he made them out: first the light song, then the mourning song, then the song for the dying. Juniper and larch below him, aspen and alder and hawthorne. All day he had chewed small stones, mixing nuts and leaves with the stones, grinding the food to a mulch. He spit the mulch in his hand. He used his free hand and a rock thumb-scraper to spoon the stink of his own leavings into the mulch, wiping the mulch on a flat stone, forming it into small round patties, watching it dry. Good, he grunted, ruminations of anguish without forbearance. Food, he'd bring it to his people. He'd carry the food down for the evening feast. He did not quite remember how they rejected him, mocking him with their fight tones when he gave, how they repelled the form of him for he kept himself from water and light, face unshapely and root-torn hair, odd lie of limbs and hands, back upturned over his shoulders, knees wide, feet narrow.

He'd left the band three winters before, and many forgot him, and most thought him dead.

Chewing his stones, he mixed his food and thought happily of evening, and thinking this way he heard again music like the sound of wind or wolf song, real voices, and the music made him lift his head and cease his work as he stared at the opening of the cave. *Nohuah,* he said quietly, Wait.

He paused on his haunches in the dark, craning his neck, bending his head toward the light. He hopped two paces forward, one to the side. The light enveloped him. Pain in the mind, stunning, he closed his eyes and turned his head to the sound, red flash and white star on the inward eye, but under everything the clarion of women singing, a young woman, and a child—and in the stillness of his own form the need arose, fruitful to him, and wicked.

FROM THE MOUTH of the cave Heavy Head emerged low, stealthy as the wolverine, quiet as the night bird, the black wing, the dayraven, and overhead echoing his path the bird on a high flight traced his line as he strode full-gaited and quick and without forethought and nearly without understanding. He honed the angle to the sound of people below, the sound so beautiful to him, and worthy he thought, to be eaten.

Walking, the young woman River Bird sang, and with her the girl-child, Dark Eye.

Neither heard his movement behind and above.

Heavy Head pounded the head of River Bird with a fist, caving the bowl of her skull, then turned and swiftly snapped Dark Eye's neck.

They fell to the forest, still-eyed, and burdenless, and he took their hair and drug their limp shapes behind him, back to the dark inside of the mountain where he devoured them, body and bones.

When the two were taken, when Heavy Head came and claimed them as his own, the Great One looked on and sent the spirit birds to lift them from their bodies and carry them to his bosom, and as they rode the evening wings their singing rose from the forest and traveled full and far, the sound reaching the father of River Bird and Dark-Eye, the man-chief Calf Robe.

And dusk came, and the sound with it, and the sound died, and a sense of alarm came to the people, and men spoke angry words and gathered beating their chests, Calf Robe and his friend Stoneshelf leading them, and rushing they ran to pursue and bring back River Bird and Dark Eye. In darkness they found the pattern of the two walkers and followed it to the place where the young woman and her sister the girl-child were forsaken, and here the men slapped and beat their bodies and viciously cried out and turned quickly and tracked the broken earth up through the young bent arms of trees, up the cliff face to the cleft in the rock.

To the sound of many feet moving Heavy Head stood deaf, as to the limp form of the women he had been mute, for to their harm he was blind, and when he had ended eating their bodies and beheld the remnant of their lightborn skeletons in the dark of the mountain, he forgot his own name, and he forgot how he had come to eat what he had eaten, slender fingers in his mouth delicate as rabbit bones.

When the men found him they pulled his body limb from limb and tore his head from his torso and lifted him and carried him from the cave and dashed all the pieces down against the rocks.

And Little Bird, mother of River Bird and Dark Eye, sat with her eyes closed in the lodge, holding her knees in her arms, facing away from the fire, crying as she rocked herself slowly forward and back.

II

HER SON

AFTER DARKNESS.

Light.

Life to the world.

In their grief, born to Little Bird and Calf Robe, a boy-child they named Blackwolf, hair full and thick the color of night, and Calf Robe's friend Stoneshelf was also as a father to the boy.

First the boy's smile was like the morning, and his crying beckoned healing, and his walking on the earth became a memory of River Bird and Dark Eye, and among her people Little Bird sang as the song-hawk, and because of the child, the people smiled again.

And still, a change came, and Little Bird foresaw the change, and even in the death of her daughters, she knew new grief would come for her and when it came, she bore it up, and doing so she gave her people peace.

Blackwolf grew and fought constantly with the other children of the band and made others afraid. Very late he listened to Calf Robe and Little Bird and tried to bow his head to the elders, Stoneshelf and the others, to sit with them in their circle, take smoke with them, and listen. But his listening was short, his obedience shorter still. Mostly, he talked and moved about, and wanted war. He pointed his face at the mountain sky. He met the world with a fist.

IN THE DARK of the lodge, the family sleeping, he woke Calf Robe and they sat together by the embers from the fire. Blackwolf's thirteenth summer.

"I weary of this place," Blackwolf said. His face grew tight. "*Hey-ehheh*. Yes father, I must go. I will ride far and hard and make something for our people." He struck his own chest with an open hand.

"*He-kohtohests!* Wait! Stay," said his father, placing his hand on Blackwolf's shoulder.

Blackwolf struck his chest again.

"You are young," said Calf Robe, seeking the boy's eyes.

Blackwolf looked away. "I am strong."

IN A NIGHT DREAM Little Bird struggled in the light between two mountains; in the air above the earth she wrestled dayraven, the Life Eater, and won.

CALF ROBE touched Blackwolf's arm. "Yes, you are strong. You must also be wise. Your sisters, your brothers in the tribe, they need you. Little Bird asks that you stay. I ask you to stay. I will train you. Wait with me."

"No, Father," said Blackwolf, and before dusk of the next day he slipped behind camp to a stand of trees and rode south and east toward the valley of three rivers, to the camp of the Sandcrane Band, to go and kill in darkness, take enemy spoil, and return home.

POWER OF *MO-EHNO-AH*, power of the horse, long stride pacing out land, black-white animal faster than wind, stronger than water, head of the beast a swift club flying. Aloft over the body of speed, Blackwolf crouched low, clutching

186

mane to hand, knees to the broad ribs of the animal, hard harmonies the intonations of horse and boy breathing, hoof beats clipped, fast, rhythmic over the plain. By night and day and night again, through a long valley that narrowed in the dark before dawn he traveled and the horse lifted him so he ascended the base of Elk Mountain north to south, grey sun hidden behind clouds on the shoulder of the earth.

Low ridge of stone. He halted and stood beside his horse, eyeing the camp of the Sandcrane Band below, the enemy, those who had killed Stoneshelf's parents long ago. Smoke from the lodges, line of three rivers lit by light, early sky overhead, opaque, illumined, and in the morning movement the Band toting water, hanging elk robes to air, some of the women already huddled using thumb-scrapers and fingers and teeth to prepare skins or begin quillwork or make ready the day's food.

Blackwolf hid his horse among cedar, trees like the gnarled hands of elders, and sat down where he would be unseen. He prayed to the Great One to be given courage and honor for his people. All day he prayed and when night came he went to his horse and rode draped on the horse's back, head low to the side, silent, slow to the camp of the Sandcrane. He rode along the river, the horse walking through tall grass to a stand of aspen not far from camp where he left the horse and traveled by foot.

From the river he approached, running in a crouch to the lodge of a chief, a big chief, an old soldier chief. He laid himself down and stilled his breath. Wind to his face, no one smelled his coming. The horses stood to the side of the lodge, three of them, all swift, two blacks and a grey, facing away from him, nudging the ground, pulling grass and lifting their heads, mane and forelock full and dark, working the jaw, the neck.

He stared at them and envisioned himself inside the soldier chief's lodge, a family of only three he'd sited from the shoulder of the mountain. He would kill the man, his wife, his child, bare hands and stone knife, feeling the flesh give way, the life exhale, then he would take the horses. He'd lead the horses to the river, back north to his own horse, over the east side of the mountain and home.

Nearly without sound he entered the lodge and stood over the sleeping form of the man and his wife. A small girl-child lay between them. He did not feel afraid as he knelt to the man to touch him, to end his life, but just as he leaned down the man turned and shouted in his face, a word direct and terrible, "*Hova-ahahnay!*": "Never!"

Blackwolf jumped back and tripped, scrambling for the entrance, breaking through, running. Black night, full of clouds. Not three strides from the opening he was hit hard in the back of the head by a stone hammer, the skull plate crushed so that he fell and his blood seeped out on the ground, and the man stood over him, screaming and beating the head and body of Blackwolf repeatedly, hammer high and swift descent, without recourse, until the man's arms were spent and he dropped to his knees, and scooped up the bones and flesh of his enemy's head and scattered the pieces far from the body.

IN THE DARK, two days away, Little Bird dreamed an echo dream of light risen over the land and she in the air above the earth, wrestling dayraven the Life Eater. The bird pecked her body, cracking her chest bone, but she held the bird by the neck and the bird succumbed to her and fell from her far and fast to the earth and broke himself on a large flat stone, and Little Bird felt great remorse. Far down, she saw dayraven's body bleed on the soil. She watched from the high place and his two wings became two rivers that flowed into one, and she became a sky of clouds pouring rain, and the river rose and the rain fell and the two met one another and covered the world.

HEAVY-HEARTED, full of fear, she woke and placed Calf Robe's arms about her, fitful until his breathing quieted her and she slept. And sleeping she dreamed again, of great gold wings outstretched over land and river, her son asleep like a child on the back-feathers of the bird, small body carried high to the home of the sun.

TO HIS HORSE the Sandcrane bound the remnant of Blackwolf's body, bruised and torn, headless, and set the horse on its way and the horse moved north along river and over mountain, through forest and over a second mountain, down to valley floor descending on a slow walk over the land along the river White-Stones-Moving to the camp of the Sichsayas.

III

LITTLE BIRD

WHEN LITTLE BIRD SAW her son she wailed and cut her arms with the longstone and tore her hair, and Calf Robe untied the boy's body, and he carried the body in his arms, and he and his friend Stoneshelf and the men of the Sichsayas set the boy's body aloft among the dead in the sacred place. When they returned to camp, Calf Robe held Little Bird, and her weeping was as the days, and her grief and her weeping a river to swell and bury the mountains. She lay in Calf Robe's arms for ten and twenty turns of the sun.

In the dark she whispered, "Will you make war?"

"No," he answered. "I am broken now."

When she rose, Calf Robe saw her eyes were as rock, and he blessed her and waved the smoke of sweetgrass over her body, her hands and face, and watched as she turned from him and began walking. She took no one and walked with only the clothes she wore to the valley of the three rivers. Calf Robe did not follow her.

SHE ENTERS THE CAMP of the Sandcrane at dawn with the sun broken over her and light in her hair and she is met by women hostile to her, who shout and drag her bodily to the center of camp. Here the Sandcrane Band looks on her with disgust, and from a near lodge she sees the soldier chief emerge, the same who had struck down and destroyed her son.

He comes and stands before her, lifting her by her hair until she also stands.

He welcomes her hatred, she sees, but she has none to give. Desolate, she kisses the chief's hand, takes and lightly kisses the underside of his wrist, and when she kisses him and lifts her face he sees her eyes are harmed and he touches her cheek and he knows that she is old and he is old and in his heart he sees the life of the women and children of the Band and he asks the Band that they might feed her and let her live with them, and they say it is good.

SHE IS GIVEN to an old woman with long grey braids, White Bear, and White Bear grabs her hair and drags her into her lodge and pushes her face down on the dirt before the fire, and speaks, "You are below us. Your son tried to kill one of our chiefs and died. Your son deserved to die." The old woman steps on Little Bird's back and stands on her, and Little Bird's air is pushed out, and she lies still as the woman talks.

"You will work twice as much as the other women. You will be our slave, yes?"

Little Bird is silent.

"Answer," says White Bear. "Yes?"

"Yes," says Little Bird.

"Now put your hand in the ashes of the fire," says the old woman, "and take eat."

"No," Little Bird answers, and nearly before the word escapes her mouth the woman is flat on top of her, wielding a small stone blade, and she cuts quickly, deftly, the corners of Little Bird's mouth, and the blood spills full and warm over Little Bird's teeth, down to the dirt.

"Eat," she says, rough in Little Bird's ear. Knife at Little Bird's eye. White Bear smells of hair and animal, of earth and the stink of breath, her teeth glinting grayish black and Little

Bird reaches into the fire and puts a handful of ash in her mouth and eats.

TWO SUMMERS FROM when she left Calf Robe, Little Bear's face slit like the coyote to a smile she cannot undo, she has made a way for herself by remaining quiet and obedient to the old woman White Bear. Mornings before dawn she gathers wood for the lodge fires, and places small bundles outside each lodge until the light comes, and outside in the shade of the old woman's lodge she sits and uses the thumbscraper to clean hides and set them to dry for robes. All day, she sews lodge skins and moccasins, breach-clouts, war-shirts, and leggings, gauntlets, baby bundles, parfleches. On White Bear's word she gathers water in the elk skin carriers, each evening for the soldier chief Runs at Night, the same who killed her son, and he watches her work and hears her silence and sees the dark red lines of the old woman's knife at her mouth.

"Why do you stay?" he asks, and she doesn't answer. She goes about her work and does what she is asked, and the people see she earns the respect of Runs at Night and his wife Bearchild.

Because of this, the young women of the Band gather and speak in low tones. "See that woman," they point with their noses.

"She eats our food."

"She takes our water."

And of an evening after Little Bird brings water to Runs at Night and Bearchild, on her way along a small rise toward White Bear's lodge, the women jump on her and push her over a small ridge and she lands awkwardly and lets out a small cry and they beat her until her head goes black and she sees no more.

LIGHTLY, SHE FEELS him lift her body and carry her to his lodge where his wife touches her wounds with water and sings to her until she sleeps. When she wakes, the fire is near and warm, and the soldier chief Runs at Night sits beside her, and his wife Bearchild touches her face.

"Be as a mother to us," he says. And she does as he asks and stays with the man Runs At Night, and his wife Bearchild. She lives in Sandcrane Band five more summers, serving Runs At Night and Bearchild, and she is loved by them, and by their daughter, the girl-child One Medicine. She learns two others, boy-children, died at birth, and she sees the great joy of Runs At Night and Bearchild when they walk with One Medicine, or as they listen to the child in the evening singing, or dance with her the round dance. Little Bird prays Runs At Night and Bearchild be given another boy-child, and she feels the place of her heart become whole again and in a dream she sees the boy-child carried on the wings of the Great Spirit to the bosom of Bearchild. And it comes to be and when the child is born Little Bird weeps, for her happiness is great, and she thanks the Great One and sings the healing song, and the light song. She gives the good songs to Sandcrane Band and the good songs soothe in her the song of mourning, the song of death.

Runs At Night and Bearchild and One Medicine smile on Little Bird, and when the boy-child comes to them they name the child Daystar after her appearing, after the sun that had brought her in the morning to the camp of the Sandcrane.

HIS NAME IS DAYSTAR, and when another summer passes they speak with Little Bird about the boy-child, and the words they speak she cannot understand, and the words rise inside Little Bird and house mountains and sky, and bring rain to the long fires, and great medicine to the Sandcrane and the Sichsayas.

Little Bird holds the child, child bound tight and warm, asleep in her arms as she rocks and sings in the lodge of Runs At Night and Bearchild.

"The Great One gives," says Bearchild, and using her lips she motions to Little Bird, and Runs At Night follows her look and sees the child in the woman's arms.

"As you have given to me," he says to Bearchild.

"As we will give," says Bearchild.

"So be it," Runs At Night answers, and his teeth shine and his thoughts greatly please him. "*Nahpehvehtahno!*"

"Yes," she says, "it pleases me too."

Little Bird rocks the child with her body, and sings the child her good songs, and her body surrounds him, warm in the lodge. She hears the sound of Runs At Night and Bearchild, words braided with her singing, and her heart becomes quiet and she and the baby sleep.

"LITTLE BIRD," Bearchild whispers, waking her.

Little Bird starts. She doesn't know where she is. Bearchild touches her hand and she grows calm. Bearchild and Runs At Night sit before her, facing her where she holds the child drawn in, the child still soundly asleep.

"Yes," she answers.

"We have met together. Runs At Night with me, and with the Band. Bearchild touches Little Bird's forehead and strokes her hair.

Soft-spoken from Bearchild, "We give you Daystar. We want you to take him back with you, to live with you among the Sichsayas. Child of peace between us. I give him to be your son, your husband to be his father."

"He is your only boy-child." Little Bird looks away.

"Yes," says Runs At Night and he points his nose to Bearchild. "We make our child your child."

CEREMONY morning to evening, four suns and four moons, and in the night of her dreams Little Bird sees the hand of the Great One reach down to touch her lips as she sleeps. On the morning of the fifth day the women dress her in finest deer-skin, feathers of the dayraven to adorn the fringe of her garment, elktooth and quillwork and red clay, feathers of the great-hawk and the gold-eagle to adorn her hair, and on her back, tailfan of the blue jay to carry the child bound there, weft of day sky for the boy-child Daystar. She sings as they prepare her, and her music fills the land and touches the mountains and kisses the sky.

She rides Fast Wind, the strongest and most gentle of Runs At Night's horses, and trails ten more, horse gifts of the Sandcrane Band to the Sichsayas, over mountain and valley, times three, back to the arms of Calf Robe.

THE BEARTOOTH RANGE

A Triptych

Panel 1

NATASHA

She was born in a clawfoot bathtub in a one room house in Red Lodge, Montana where farms sit high in a valley and the mountains open like the mouth of a bear and the wind is a message that speaks your name. The year was 1934. She with the stride of the wolverine, speed in the mountains like a natural wonder and love in the heart like a bird in the hand, a miracle of body and breath capable of song and flight in equal measure. In the Beartooths where mighty rock meets open sky she lived brightly alive, her beauty a swath of sun at dusk, a vision to both old and young.

Her name was Natasha Bahktin.

She tamed deer with her touch.

Her voice soothed the bear cub.

Her father was a flamethrower in World War II.

Her mother beaded moccasins she sold to the rich whites of the east.

Half Cheyenne, half Russian, Natasha grew tall and danced like a wild new creature, her body an altar, her face and eyes striking. Her way in the world of men, quick and incisive.

IN THE WINTER of '67 to the despair of the citizens of Red Lodge, Natasha died.

On Christmas day, at the age of thirty-three, the truck she drove slid through a high embankment in a whiteout and went airborne. The vehicle hit the ice of the river below and broke through.

Natasha's death haunted the town for years and made people weep when a big snow fell as they huddled in their homes against the cold.

Terrible, the old women muttered to themselves, shaking their heads.

In spring the people found her in the red heart of the cherry blossoms, a grieving they bore in the chest and the eyes, but there was one who grieved more than the others, whose grief took a long time going. Closer than a sister, Jane Hirsch lived a long life. Fifty winters after the truck was found awash in the basin, Jane addressed her final diary entry to Natasha on the first day of spring.

PANEL 2

JANE

Sister of my heart, I am eighty-three now. My grown children, my two daughters, sleep in chairs at the foot of the bed. My youngest granddaughter rests in my arms, a child only five years old whose voice reminds me of you.

Every time I hold her I remember.

You gave me strength.

I miss you.

I've tried to give my children the same strength.

Your mother passed just before I moved to town. You bore sorrows none of us knew. Your father already gone, I remember you were adopted by the old woman who lived in the cabin out toward Two Oceans Plateau.

You befriended me, the new girl who needed a friend.

Same age and birthday. One soul, I like to think.

The cancer hurts my hands, but I write now to leave this legacy for my daughters. I count them as your daughters too. I want them to see their task in this world is to love without measure.

Just three years before you died, when my husband and only son were killed in the train wreck at Wolfpoint you watched my life go dark. I was lost and found no light. But you were there.

Saying nothing, you arrived each day and rubbed my feet.

Wearing the knitted shawl my mother gave against the chill, you touched my feet and let me weep. Blew heat into your hands and took my stocking feet and put pressure into the arch.

As the months passed, you were present with me in a grief I thought would never end. My tears emptied me and finally in the heart of that darkness the imprint of your touch was irrevocable.

"You have two other children," you said. "Come back. They need you."

So I returned, and I'm still here.

With touch everything is acknowledged.

My grief has turned to happiness, Tasha.

I feel lucky now. My granddaughter bears your name.

My son and my husband watch over me from heaven.

In my bed, I look out on these mountains.

At dusk they burn like fire.

Today, I place my diary next to yours on the windowsill. When I'm gone my family will read our final entries, mine dated today, yours from your last day in this world, when you mentioned you had something important to tell me, something ultimate.

Not long until I see you, my friend.

Love is stronger than death.

PANEL 3

NATASHA SPEAKS TO GOD

Jane approaches, only a moment from yesterday.

God of my unknowing, You breathe the stars into being.

She too has been annihilated. Her life, as mine, has been annihilated.

Her beauty, as mine, reborn.

We were fragmented and disintegrated, only to be reconstituted here, more beautiful than before. What is the meaning of father? She knew and led me to You even without my knowing, until at last I knew, and then You took me home. I drove along high mountain roads to her house, but I was taken into the sky, and it was then I saw as Hopkins saw, the fire that breaks from Thee, a billion times told lovelier, more dangerous, oh my Beloved.

I have missed her with an infinite longing.

But my heart remembers. Thank You for memory.

We followed her father everywhere. Our heroes the basketball players who starred for her father's team at Plenty Coup: young men with names that rang of joy and abandon: Charles Falls Down, Edmond Roundface, Russell Pretty Horse. We loved them on those long bus rides in the dark after we left the light of gymnasiums that pulsed and rumbled with the heat of people and popcorn. The lacquered shine of hardwood floors.

We hunted and fished with her father too, and later on our own. My heart is full from those days when our lives seemed held together in a gold-red tapestry.

We walked with giants of forest and stone.

Silven Lake at the top of the mountains where blue water mirrors sky.

Land of grizzlies and black bears, mountain goats and bighorns, elk and moose and wolverine. Land formed of Your hand. Lovely land of our wanderings through spruce and whitebark pine, lodgepole, and grasses, untold wildflowers with their blooms set toward Island Lake or Lonesome Peak, Mystic and East Rosebud.

Then she knew but a pale light. Now she will know in full.

Creator, what more have you given us to know?

These events for which my life was made forfeit.

These events, unfolding before us.

Our wait is the blink of an eye. We would know all in that flash of light.

There on the windowsill, she has left my journal with hers, for her children.

Of my own story, whatever good it gives: Word of God, speak.

MY FATHER left for the great war when I was five. When he came back two years later he left again, fractured in heart and mind, and didn't return. My mother wore the marks of his rage. She was alone and a seamstress and she loved me and I loved her. But he was gone, and for a time I despised my life.

He never wrote, never called.

"Gone to New York," my mother said, bruising her lips with lipstick.

Abandoned, I thought, and I hated him.

It was like he was dead or we were dead.

When I was twelve my mother died of lung cancer and I was scared my father would come back. But I waited and he never came and that was even worse.

Before you arrived, Jane, I loved death too much.

The first time my father and I talked on the phone I was nineteen.

A strange, awkward conversation. Not much talking involved.

Silence and hesitation. Not knowing.

He called Mrs. Oliver, my legal guardian. We sat in her kitchen at the metal table with the white Formica top. He called her in a drunken stupor, saying, "I want my daughter back." She told me who it was and handed me the phone. I took the call because of you. He said, "I love you, Natasha." His voice slurred and he was searching, like he wanted me to say, *I love you too, Dad.* But I didn't have it in my heart. I just said, "I have to go now," and said goodbye, and he swore and slammed the phone down.

He was a stranger to me.

The words *I love you* would have been empty. They would have meant nothing.

I kept silent then. But you helped me more than you know. I was nineteen when he tried to make contact, twelve years since he left. That was not the first time I had tried to make contact though. In the seventh grade you and I went to Clydehurst Ranch near Bozeman for dance and voice. An instructor there saw the anger in me. She told me, "What you hate is what you become." Knowing I hated my dad, and knowing he was an alcoholic and the fact that I'm Northern Cheyenne and my mom taught me to stay away from alcohol, I feared I might become just like him if I kept hating.

So I wrote him a letter.

202

I could have done a better job of saying what I did but it was the best way I knew how. When I met you, you loved me despite my fears. Your family, and especially you. We were so young, so new to each other. I never told you about the letter. I didn't want you to be ashamed of me, and years later when I saw you climb the mountain of sorrow left by the death of your husband and son, I watched and felt wrecked. But watching you helped me get some goodness back in my life about my father. When I was nineteen though, there were so many things that still needed to be settled. I had never once said *I love you* to my father. I'd said *I forgive you* in that letter, but I couldn't bring myself to love him.

I believed I could forgive him, but that didn't mean I had to love him.

But the Mystery takes us, doesn't it?

God touches the mountains and they smoke.

Love does not let go. I never told you how much you healed me.

The car was lost to gravity, my words in your world went silent.

After my father contacted me only two or three times between the ages of nineteen and thirty-three, an opportunity came for me to see him. I never told you that either. I was still too held by shame.

His older brother was getting married in Billings. A month before the wedding my father called to say he'd be there. I was fearful. But I knew now I needed to be able to approach him because of how you, your whole family, had loved me. I didn't reveal my plan to you because I was afraid I wouldn't be able to follow through and I'd look like a fool again.

There were so many years there, and between you and your family's touch on me so much gradual healing took place. I had come to terms with much of the loss. I had been given a home. I had been blessed with Mrs. Oliver who cared for me, provided for me, gave me opportunities to succeed in life, and I had been around you. I started to believe in myself and not be ashamed but rather to accept and be proud of my past, my heritage.

But I was still afraid.

My father called and said he was coming, and he showed up in Billings four weeks later. And during those four weeks, in between the time he called and the wedding, I prayed every night in the way you and I always prayed, simply, with a whole and broken heart: *God, I really need your help, I need you because I don't have any love for him. I want to be able to say I love you to him. So I ask for Your love so I can show him love.*

I prayed this prayer every night until the wedding.

And the whole time, you were with me.

In the end he came to see his brother and I went down to Billings to meet him. I was taken aback by his appearance. I remembered him as a child would, when I was seven years old—that was the last time I'd seen him. I remembered him young and powerful, when he had black hair and he was tall with a beautiful face. Being Russian and from Montana he had rough skin and dark eyes, and to me he was a prince of a man.

But when I saw him at the wedding I was startled.

His eyes held so much pain. He was haggard. There was no light in him. His brother was getting married. His daughter had come to see him. He should have rejoiced. But he was hardened. Like he had no heart left. He was bent over at the neck and shoulders. His hair was grey. He'd been handsome. Now he stooped when he walked. There was no confidence in him. That weekend we spent about six or seven hours together. I smelled alcohol on his breath always. The night after the wedding we went back to his motel room. He had to pick up some clothes, and when I walked into the room it smelled like a liquor store. Even his skin carried the stench of alcohol, of hard liquor, the same that was on his breath. I walked out of his room and just said to myself, *It's nothing, nothing to concern yourself with. Give him grace. Let him be.*

The next day he was leaving and it was mid-morning.

I stood in the tiny front room of the motel. Everyone was there to say their goodbyes, and he was nervous. He was hesitant. He shifted back and forth, and I was also nervous. I prayed the whole time to myself, *I'm going to be strong, I'm going to be strong.* I was ready to cry. He stood across the room, and I stood and faced him. He hadn't been a part of my life for so long, he'd had no real contact, and it was too long since he'd heard the words *I love you* from my lips. I could see he was scared. He was afraid of many things. We'd never talked openly about his alcohol, it was a skirted issue. Then he said, "Well, I've got to be going now, I have a long road ahead of me. I have to get back east." He tried to make small talk, but the words fell away and he went silent. He didn't know what to say. I took three steps and walked across the room and put my arms out, and when he took a step toward me I wrapped him in my arms.

"I love you, Dad," I said.

His hair was near my face, our faces touched.

He was real close. I had my hands on his back and I drew him in and held him. I made sure it felt strong, not weak.

I said, "I love you."

I let go of all I'd held against him.

Jane, without you that day would have never occurred.

I am filled with love. If I gave my father something, I gave him his daughter back, giving my heart to him as a daughter

205

and looking at him as my father. I was on my way to tell you. I hope you know the life you gave him and me.

The heart is a house of joy!

TODAY, I see you not as through a glass darkly, but face to face.

I reach and hold your hand.

The mountains in winter are cathedrals, and even now if we rise on the wings of the dawn and if we settle on the far side of the waters, we are not alone. If we touch the stars and walk on the winds of the firmament, even there you are with me.

Do not be afraid.

We are not cold and far apart.

We are not abandoned.

We are beloved.

ABOUT THE AUTHOR

Poet, short story writer, and novelist Shann Ray grew up in Montana and Alaska and spent part of his childhood on the Northern Cheyenne reservation. His work has been featured in *Poetry, Esquire, McSweeney's, Prairie Schooner, Big Sky Journal, Narrative,* and *Salon.* A National Endowment for the Arts Fellow and winner of the American Book Award and the High Plains Book Award, he is the author of *American Masculine, American Copper, Atomic Theory 432, Balefire, Sweetclover,* and *Forgiveness and Power in the Age of Atrocity.* A clinical psychologist specializing in the psychology of men, he teaches leadership and forgiveness studies at Gonzaga University. Because of his wife and three daughters he believes in love.

ABOUT THE PRESS

Unsolicited Press is a small press in Portland, Oregon. The small press is fueled by voracious editors, all of whom are volunteers. The press began in 2012 and continues to produce stellar poetry, fiction, and creative nonfiction.

Learn more at www.unsolicitedpress.com.